VICKI FINDS THE ANSWER

The CHERRY AMES Stories

☆　　☆　　☆

The VICKI BARR Flight Stewardess Series

"You're running away," Vicki guessed. Joan nodded miserably.

Vicki Finds the Answer

VICKI FINDS THE ANSWER

BY HELEN WELLS

GROSSET & DUNLAP
PUBLISHERS
New York

CONTENTS

VICKI FINDS THE ANSWER

CHAPTER I

New York

NEW YORK GLISTENED IN THE SUN THIS FINE AUTUMN Sunday.

"What a city!" Vicki exulted to herself. She put her finger on the doorbell of the apartment she shared with five other flight stewardesses, and rang. "And to think now I live right here in the heart of New York!"

Vicki switched her overnight bag to her other hand, and rang again. "Aren't any of those rascals up yet? Or are all my colleagues out on flights? Where's my key?"

The door opened suddenly and a tomboyish young woman in a bathrobe made a lunge for Vicki.

"Jean!" Vicki hugged her. "Did I wake you up?"

"Welcome home! How is Fairview, Illinois? Did you have a good rest?" Vicki's fair head and Jean Cox's cropped brown one were close as they clung together, laughing. "No, you didn't wake me up. But the others are still in the yawning stage. We're all home at once, for once. Come on in."

1

"Chatterbox. How are you?"

The two girls went in and dropped Vicki's bag in the deserted living room. Jean bounced down on the couch, her bare feet stuck straight out in front of her like a small boy's.

"Let's have a look at you, Vicki Barr!"

Vicki smiled rather shyly, took off her hat, and ran her fingers through her soft ash-blonde hair. She was small and slight, with a delicate air.

Jean chuckled. "If I didn't know you, I'd think you were as sissy as you look."

Vicki winked one angelic blue eye. "I'll have you know I'm a full-fledged, professional flight stewardess, with all of two months' flying and one measly assignment behind me! Tell me, did you hear yet—"

"I'll bet everybody wants to protect you," Jean teased.

"They do, and then they're put out when they find I don't need protecting." Vicki's sensitive little face crinkled up with mischief. "Now tell me! Did word leak out yet of what my new assignment is to be?"

"Not yet, sweetie. But we're going to celebrate tonight, anyhow!"

"Hurray, a party," Vicki said with satisfaction. "A New York party! Who's responsible? Dean and company?"

"Of course. Arranged on purpose so you'd be back for it. Hey, Vicki, know what I did while you were gone? I borrowed your friend Dean Fletcher's Piper Cub, down south, and flew 'er around to my heart's content. Oh, bliss."

Vicki awarded her a left-hand salute. "Jean Cox of the Flying Coxes. Aren't you somepin'!"

"Vic, you simply must learn to pilot a plane—even if I have to teach you myself. That's a promise. Or a threat." Jean stretched and wiggled her toes. "Have to get showered and dressed, now. Excuse me, will you? Don't be lonesome."

Left by herself in the comfortable living room, Vicki perched on the window sill, looking down on Central Park, and congratulated herself. She was still amazed and overjoyed about this whole adventure. Only last spring, a sophomore at the State University, she had been quietly living with her professor father, her mother, and her little sister Ginny, in The Castle in Fairview. Now, this autumn, she was on her own—a graduate of the Federal Airlines Stewardess School— proud possessor of a career in the clouds—with a host of new friends—sharing this home-base apartment with some of the girls she had trained with—and facing the prospect of flying anywhere in the world.

"It's almost too good to be true." Vicki rubbed her cheek against the cold windowpane. "Now if I could only see an air map marked with my new route—and with my future!"

She had only until tomorrow morning to wait for

that. Meanwhile she could dream. Dreams for Vicki meant flying—and the strange, beautiful world of the sky.

"Vicki? Didn't I hear Vicki come in?"

Charmion Wilson came running in. She always reminded Vicki of a gentle-eyed doe. She was fair and sweet-faced, a little taller and older than the other stewardesses.

"How was the vacation? You look so well!"

Vicki put an affectionate arm around Charmion.

"The vacation was fine, and my dad's cooking this time—it's his hobby, you know—was sensational. How're you? What's been happening to you?" Vicki asked with concern.

"I've started on a new flight route." Charmion's gentle face lighted. "It's only to Boston, but it's interesting. A complete change of scene. I guess you and I are the only new stewardesses who won new runs."

They smiled at each other. Vicki said, "Boston should be delighted to have you."

Vicki was pleased that Charmion had received the encouragement and stimulus of a new assignment. She needed it. Only a few months ago, Charmion's flier husband had been killed in a ground accident. Charmion had gone into aviation work in order to keep Hank Wilson's name alive.

"Have you had your breakfast, Vicki?"

"Not yet."

"I'll get it for you. Our Mrs. Duff won't be in for another hour."

"Thanks, but why should you wait on me? I'll get my breakfast myself, Mrs. Wilson."

Charmion moved off toward the kitchen. "Oh, I'm getting nourishment for us all. Almost ready. You know perfectly well I'm the only housewife in our midst."

"Want a willing if not-so-efficient helper?"

"No, dear, you've had a long trip. You rest. Besides, you'd only be in my way." Charmion smiled and disappeared.

Vicki had no immediate chance to rest. The fragrance of coffee brought Dotty and Tessa, via an eviction from the kitchen, bursting into the living room.

Dot Crowley had red hair, a square jaw, and a strong, confident voice. Tessa, who had originally trained to go on the stage, was dark and dramatic in a crimson negligee. These two already were engaged in one of their customary arguments. They stopped long enough to greet Vicki and welcome her back into the fold.

The redhead grinned. "We missed your soothing presence."

"You would," Vicki said ruefully.

"Yes," said Tessa tartly. "Our Big Executive needs a little toning down."

"What about you? Prima donna!" Dot shot back.

Laughing, Vicki waved her white handkerchief. "Truce, truce! What's the battle about this time?"

Dot Crowley looked slightly ashamed of herself. "Oh, I'm soapboxing for executive ability, as *the* way to get ahead, and Tessa's holding out for personality."

"Personality plus!"

"Plus what?"

"Plus—plus—" Tessa threw up her arms in a wide gesture of disgust. "Just because *you* haven't got a spotlight personality!"

Dot sputtered as if she wanted to explode but was trying hard not to.

"Hold tight, Dotty." Vicki grinned. "Count to ten. Count to two hundred and seventy-three. In fractions."

The redheaded girl flung herself down on the couch. "Well, no one can say I'm not holding onto my temper—"

"—and your overaggressiveness," Tessa put in, redraping the crimson negligee.

"—but Tessa ought to stop provoking me!"

"I? I provoke anybody?" Tessa looked up and gave a beautifully modulated laugh. "Why, at rehearsals in dramatic school, everyone said I wasn't a bit temperamental."

Vicki sighed and sat down beside Dotty. "How you two do enjoy quarreling with each other! It's really one of the most satisfying friendships these old eyes have ever seen. Ah, me."

Both girls looked sheepish, then slowly began to grin.

They were discussing Vicki's new shoes, very high-heeled as usual, and whether she did (or did not) look more sophisticated, when little Celia Trimble came straggling in. Celia stopped rubbing her eyes, and her china-doll face beamed at Vicki.

"I declare! She's home. I thought I heard Jean say so but I'm so sleepy I couldn't be certain." Celia's treble was soft and southern. "Charmion says, is everybody having pancakes, and how many can you eat, or not?"

The other girls blinked a little at Celia's *non sequitur*. Vicki decided to reply in kind.

"Yes," said Vicki.

Celia nodded, finding this an adequate answer. "Dotty?"

Dot groaned. "No pancakes for Crowley. Crowley gets fat. The airline warned me that if I gain another five pounds they'll ground me until I stop overloading the plane."

Tessa admitted she was in the same fix.

Celia trotted back to the kitchen with this bulletin. Vicki kindly offered to eat Tessa's and Dot's pancakes for them, since she could outeat them all, with no visible results. Tessa and Dot bitterly requested her not to bring up that fact.

Breakfast was a scramble. With Charmion and Celia bringing in trays of food, Vicki hurriedly set the big table in the window, Tessa dragged over chairs, and

Dot directed proceedings. "From your place on the couch," Tessa commented. "Oh, for the life of an executive." They were all seated around the table, more or less on top of one another, when Jean came in whistling.

Jean was dressed now, but still barefoot. She announced delightedly, "I've just discovered how good it feels without shoes and stockings. My feet really appreciate it. Move over, Vicki."

Vicki moved over, and she and Jean perched together on the one remaining chair.

"Who'll have what?" Charmion asked. "Shall I serve, or is it every woman for herself?"

"Bare feet are no discovery," said Dot. "I knew all about that when I was little. Also, all about the glories of wading in puddles after it's rained."

"Who tacked up that big sign in the hall: SOUP?"

"I did," stated Celia. "To remind Mrs. Duff."

"Hasn't anybody," Vicki started hopefully, "heard what my new route—"

Jean stopped her. "You and Charmion with new runs. You two teacher's pets. And you, Vic, the baby of the class, the youngest stewardess—"

"Baby—had to bring a letter of permission from her parents!"

"Stop it!" Vicki turned pink to the tips of her ears. "Speak to the stork. It's not *my* fault!"

"—while the rest of us plug along on the same old routes we've had since graduation."

"What are we going to wear to the party tonight?" Tessa shrilled over everyone else. "*Please* let's wear long dresses!"

They sidetracked into a heated debate about clothes. Vicki waited for a lull, then tried again.

"About my new route—" she began.

Celia turned confidingly to her. "Did you know I'm trying for the Babies' Plane? It's my dream. It's a special plane, nobody but babies get to ride on it. And their mothers. I'd feed them milk—out of special bottles—"

"Who, the mothers?"

"No, just the babies," Celia answered seriously. "And there are hammock cribs, and special baby foods, and—well, I adore babies anyhow."

Dot tossed her red head and snorted.

"Ignore our Big Executive," said Tessa, eyes flashing.

"Celia," said Vicki judicially, "is a girl who knows what she likes and works at it. If she doesn't get that assignment, I'll eat Dot's red hair. About my new run, now—"

"The calf! Tell Vicki about the calf!"

Jean's tanned face crinkled. "I had a very small, pedigreed calf for a passenger. Riding in the cargo compartment along with the mail, and so lonesome that the poor little thing cried."

"Jean went back there and they held hooves," Charmion teased.

"I went back there and fed it milk out of one of those baby bottles. Ever play nursemaid to a calf, two miles up in an electric storm? Anything can happen to a flight stewardess. Anything."

"We're all going to learn to make up berths, for night flights!"

"My route, my new route," Vicki muttered sadly. She wanted to know, too, who her pilot and copilot were to be.

"Just in case I do get the nursery plane," Celia was saying, "they gave me a talking-to about kidnapings."

"Did you see in the newspaper the other day where the police caught a narcotics ring operating through an airline?"

"Yes," Jean Cox said. "Well," she added, shrugging, "you never know whom you're carrying or what they're up to. As Vicki knows."

Vicki nodded, thinking of her recent adventure.

There was a sudden, glum silence. Then the conversation went headlong, on the topic of mysteries in the air, veered back to tonight's party, and was in full cry on the subject of tonight's masculine escort—when someone loudly clanged for attention.

It was Mrs. Duff, their roly-poly housekeeper. She was standing in the living-room doorway and beating on a pie tin with a spoon, to make herself heard over the girls' clamor.

"There's a man dead in Glasgow and ye're making sufficient noise to awaken him. May we not have a wee speck o' peace and quiet here? After all, it's the Lord's day."

Mrs. Duff came over to the table and started to clear away their breakfast dishes.

"Ah, Mrs. Duff," the girls teased her, "you're not really annoyed with us, are you?"

"No, I have not the heart, but I wish I might be annoyed with ye. Of the many batches of flight stewardesses I've mothered, ye six are the noisiest! Of all the fracas, uproar, and bombilation!"

They were not sure what "bombilation" was, but they melted away amid giggles.

Vicki telephoned a telegram to her family to let them know she had arrived safely in New York. Then she went off to the bedroom she shared with Jean and Charmion. She changed into her blue housecoat, unpacked, and hung away, also, her blue flight uniform. She touched the sleeve as it hung there, and the silver wings pinned at the breast pocket. A thrill of anticipation welled up in her at the thought of the new run. It would be fun if she drew Dean Fletcher as her copilot again. They had genuinely enjoyed working together last summer. Well, she would see Dean this evening—perhaps he would know what the fates, in the shape of Federal Airlines, held in store for them both.

"If he'll tell me," Vicki thought. "He'll probably give me a lecture on radar instead."

But she remembered that Dean was a wonderful dancing partner and, humming, Vicki took out her dress for the evening. Since she owned only one long frock, a filmy black chiffon with billowing sleeves, the problem of what to wear was neatly solved. Vicki examined the dress, to avoid any nth-hour scramble for needle and thread, and decided on the golden slippers and gold handbag to go with it. Her short white kid gloves. Earrings— No, they pinched.

"Open the door, please!"

Vicki sprang to the door. Charmion eased through, holding high a freshly pressed, pale-gray satin gown.

"Oh! Lovely!" Vicki exclaimed.

"It was my wedding dress. I decided there was no reason not to use it, so I had it tinted."

Jean galloped in at that moment bearing a bright red dress. She waved it before them like a cape before a bull. "They'll notice me in this! Boy, nobody could miss seeing red—and Cox in it!"

"Just whom," Charmion inquired with a twinkle, "do you want to notice you?"

"Oh—nobody in particular."

"Really?" Vicki cocked an azure eye. "You've curled your hair, too. First time I ever saw you do that."

"Next you'll think I'm eloping—just because I powdered my nose!"

"Are you eloping?"

"No! Unfortunately."

They laughed and Jean, thinking herself unobserved, blew out a sigh of relief. But Vicki's enormous blue eyes which saw everything—despite their dreamy air—noted that sigh, too. She impishly started them talking of their escorts for the evening.

This was not a matter of individual dates; rather, they were to go as a group, six girls and six boys. Vicki was glad of the group arrangement, because it spared Charmion's feelings, and because without it one or two of the girls might not have been asked for a date.

Vicki had another reason for preferring it. She was blessed, or handicapped, by having two admirers, flier Dean Fletcher and the young newspaperman Peter Carmody. Pete complained long and loud that Vicki gave Dean most of her time, and their work did throw Vicki and Dean together a good deal. But she liked Pete too. He amused her because he was full of a wry kind of mischief and did odd things, like keeping a monkey named Bernard Shaw. Vicki giggled at the thought.

"What's funny?" said Jean Cox.

"Oh, I was just thinking about Bernard Shaw."

"I don't see . . . Oh, you mean Pete's monkey," Jean Cox said. "You know, Vicki, Pete has always liked you, but you've never seemed to respond."

"That's because Vic likes Dean," Charmion called

from the depths of the closet. "Admit it, Vicki."

"I like Pete well enough, and I have not gone overboard for Dean, or for anybody," Vicki stated firmly.

"You don't appreciate Pete Carmody," Jean accused her. "I always thought he was fun."

"Perhaps I don't appreciate his many sterling virtues, madam. But don't bother feeling sorry for Pete. He's not so interested in me as all that."

"Hmm," said Jean.

Charmion emerged from the closet. "I propose we all take walks and/or naps, so we'll be beautiful for this evening."

Vicki agreed that the best beauty treatment is good health, but she declined to take a walk, even though it meant a promenade along Fifth Avenue with the festive Sunday crowds.

"I'll settle for a nap instead," she decided.

The nap turned into a good, long sleep. It was six when Vicki awoke. Charmion and Jean—"those great walkers!"—were fast asleep on the twin beds on either side of her. Vicki shook them awake.

"Six o'clock! The boys are calling for us at eight! And it will take us hours to dress!"

Mrs. Duff insisted on giving them supper first, which they bolted down, too excited to be hungry, then plunged into dressing for a gala evening. Tessa made a major chore of it. She stayed so long in the bathtub, giving herself a facial, that Vicki and Celia threatened to toss her out.

"Next time we take an apartment," Tessa wailed, as she stumbled out in towels with mud pack on her face, "we'll get one with two or three bathrooms!"

"I can't wait that long for a bath," Vicki said, and got herself scrubbed in a hurry.

Charmion's fair hair was in a tangle and Vicki patiently combed it out for her. Dot Crowley, who pretended to scorn boys, was so excited that she spilled perfume down the whole front of her dress. The entire troupe hastily improvised something else for her to wear. After the clock had spun around another half hour, they had the redhead arrayed in Tessa's extra evening skirt and a lace blouse of Celia's.

"It's a tight fit," Celia cautioned. "Don't take any deep breaths."

"Looks better than my own dress," said Dot, not a bit remorseful at having delayed them all.

Vicki was padding around in her long slip, searching for stockings. The pair she had just put on had a run, and her box of stockings had disappeared. She found them, after an exasperating hunt, not in the drawer where they should have been, but in the closet resting on her shoe rack.

"Why, Vicki," Charmion reminded her, "you put the stocking box there yourself, so you couldn't forget where it was!"

"But I forgot to remind myself to remember. Heavens, is that the doorbell already?"

"Don't tell me the boys are here so soon! Didn't any

of them get stuck in his stiff shirt?" Jean sputtered.

"If my brother arrives too early," Tessa shouted from the adjoining bedroom, "I'll never forgive him!"

Mrs. Duff, closing the door again, reassured them that it was only a telegram for Vicki. Startled, Vicki ran to open it. She hoped there was nothing wrong at home, nor anything to keep her away from tonight's party. The telegram read: "You forgot your rubbers. Shall I mail them or did you forget them on purpose? Love, Mother."

Vicki sat down in relief. But Charmion prodded her to get ready. She brushed her silver-blonde hair into a halo, spread a big handkerchief over her coiffure, and slipped into her dress. She emerged with not a hair out of place. Another dab of powder on her nose. The corsage of tiny silk rosebuds tucked into her belt. Perfume. Bag. Gloves. There, she was ready.

She went out into the living room where all six girls were congregating.

"You look exquisite, Vicki!"

"We all look pretty special!"

Celia wore a bouffant, puff-sleeved dress that managed to suggest southern moonlight and jasmine. Tessa was expectedly theatrical in slim, tight-sleeved, perfectly plain white, striking with her mane of dark hair. Dot, gingerly striding around in the borrowed lace blouse and skirt, looked positively handsome. A bombshell effect was what Jean Cox had achieved. The best surprise was Charmion, touchingly lovely in the gray gown. They all complimented Charmion, admired one another, and hoped their escorts would approve, too.

"Fortunately none of our colors clash," Vicki observed. She turned on one toe to make her dress float.

"It's raining," Mrs. Duff grumbled. "Girls, ye'll have to wear overshoes."

"We'd as soon wear long red underwear!" they overruled her.

The six of them settled down in the living room, careful not to muss skirts, to wait for the boys to arrive. Dean, Pete, Tessa's brother, two of his friends Don and Jerry, and a second young copilot, Bill Boyd, were coming. Except Bill, they all frequently dropped in at the apartment, to dance to radio music and raid the icebox—and to be shooed home by Mrs. Duff promptly at ten.

Five minutes went by.

"Aren't they ever coming?"

"My perfume isn't going to last."

Vicki sneezed and applied her handkerchief. "Oh, dear, now the powder's off my nose."

"Vicki!" Mrs. Duff called. "Wear your overshoes!"

Another five minutes went by. The girls fidgeted.

"Are you sure this is the right evening?"

"Maybe Dean and Bill were called out on flights!"

Charmion pointed out that, after all, it was not yet eight o'clock.

The doorbell rang. They jumped. Mrs. Duff admitted Dean Fletcher. He poked his head in and said, "Well, just look! And they can fly, too." Vicki went into the hall with him, to get him a coat hanger.

"Nice timing. I would have to be the first one to get here."

"Do not fear. I shall protect you!"

Dean smiled down at her out of serious gray eyes. "How are you, Vic?"

"Very well indeed." She watched the young airman as he hung away his coat. Open admiration would not have done, for the thoroughly masculine Dean—one of five brothers and no sisters—embarrassed easily. He was a nice-looking boy, rangy, with a long stride, and a flier's clear, steady, impersonal eyes.

"All set for tomorrow morning's new run?"

"I can hardly wait. But I don't know what route it's to be! Dean, do you know?"

"Sorry." But he grinned.

Tessa's brother Bob, with his friends Don and Jerry, arrived next. The girls had dubbed them The Three Bears because of their varying heights—"medium, tall, and out of sight." They were still in college, nice boys, good company, and given to turning highbrow unless squelched. Now, they refused to part with their coats.

"We'll be starting right out anyway. We have tickets for the ice show. Where are Pete and—what's-his-name?—Boyd. That's an eight-thirty curtain."

"Sorry we couldn't take you to dinner. But we're going to the Fountain Room for dancing and supper after the show."

The girls exclaimed with delight. Dean went off in a corner with Bob, presumably to discuss the evening's arrangements. Tessa tried to listen in, sister-fashion, but Bob chased her away.

Bill Boyd rang their doorbell. He was a husky blond boy with a wide grin: he looked like a football player. None of them knew him very well, but Dean had invited this copilot and vouched for him. Bill seemed a little shy, in the face of all the rapid introductions, and Vicki went to his rescue.

"Hello! I'm the one named Vicki. How come I've never seen you out at the airfield?"

"Different schedules, I guess. But I've seen you."

"Have you? Well, say hello next time."

Bill Boyd grinned. "I'll wave, too. Say, I hope I can dance well enough to suit you ladies."

"If you really get stuck, I'll teach you, sir."

"That a Hoosier twang I hear in your voice, Vicki?"

"I'm from Fairview, Illinois, pardner."

"Kinnickkinnick, Ohio, ma'am."

"There's no such place!" Vicki challenged him. "You're making it up!"

Bill chuckled. "There is too such a place. Just above Chillicothe, a few farms and a creek. One of the farms is my family's." He was still chuckling. "No such place, she says! It's an Indian name."

"All right, pardner. Shake."

They shook hands, laughing. Vicki had a new friend. And Bill Boyd seemed more at ease.

The last one Mrs. Duff admitted was Pete Carmody. He was the complete extrovert, with a rakish air. Vicki sometimes wondered if that air and his cherished, carefully battered old hat were not Pete's attempts to glamorize his role as reporter. His eyes sparkled as he saw all the gay gowns. Jean, to Vicki's surprise, went to receive him. But Pete was not permitted to take his coat off.

"Get your coats on, everybody!" Bob directed. "Don and I'll go downstairs and corral some cabs."

CHAPTER II

Party

THEY DROVE TO THE THEATER BETWEEN SHEER CLIFFS OF buildings, along crowded, brightly lighted, rain-shiny streets. Even rain was spectacular in New York. They climbed out of their cabs under a marquee, and made their way through a crowded, brilliant lobby.

The usher showed them to seats well forward in the orchestra section. The twelve of them filled nearly a whole row. Vicki sat down beside Bill Boyd, and Dean followed her. She saw that Jean and Pete were sitting next to each other, away off on the end.

The band struck up a medley of songs from the show. No one seemed to listen, but went right on talking instead. Then the lights dimmed—too soon for Vicki, who found the vivacious, gaily dressed New York audience a whole show in itself.

The curtain slowly, softly went up on a scene of crystal beauty—a ballet poised on ice, in costumes of white and silver. It was so lovely that the audience

21

involuntarily applauded. The music gave a sudden burst and the frozen tableau came to life, dancers skimming and darting on their skates like birds.

Vicki loved it. Dancing was one of her hobbies, and to see all this grace plus whirlwind skating took her breath away. The company had flawless professional skill. They leaped, spun, cavorted, fifty of them in perfect rhythm, lightly and effortlessly.

Clowns came next, three men in baggy pants and huge red wigs. They wobbled on their skates, stumbled over barrels, tripped across one another—all with an air of injured surprise. The audience howled.

Then, with a fanfare, came the première danseuse. She whirled out on the stage so fast she looked like a flashing pillar of diamonds. Suddenly she stopped stock-still on the point of one skate, smiled, and curtsied to the audience, holding out her brief spangled skirt. Then she floated into a dance.

After the intermission, the ballerina came on again, accompanied by two partners, and then the whole ballet. All of them were dressed in ermine and hats with white plumes, which blew as they skated. More ballet, as butterflies with enormous fragile wings, as children in crinolines. A fast and furious jazz number followed. Then the clowns returned in scrubwomen's clothes, playing ice hockey with mops, buckets, and a big bar of soap. Twice more the star danced: in an ice blue production number and, for a finale, an underseas fantasy.

Vicki could have watched indefinitely, but the performance was over. Dean had to pry her out of her seat.

"Stop dreaming, Vic. We're going on to the Fountain Room."

She reluctantly got to her feet, murmuring, "I'm going to try some of those dance routines on the lake at home, when it freezes over. The butterfly one—"

"You are going to put your coat on, just now. Remember?"

"Oh, yes." Vicki came back to reality with a thump.

They drove through tall streets packed with theater crowds, to one of Manhattan's famous hotels. As their party walked through the lounges and lobbies, Dean had to prod Vicki again. She was fascinated by the people standing and coming and going, by the gorgeous salons, by the flowers, furs and jewels, luggage, by the sound of French behind her and Spanish at her elbow, by the laughter and music and dozens of phones softly ringing and uniformed staff people hurrying— Dean had to take her by the hand and lead her.

Up ahead of her, Pete and Jean Cox turned around. "Don't you *want* to have supper and dance?" Jean asked.

"Yes, but—but—" Vicki was so excited she stuttered. "Everything comes so fast! It's so lavish—there's so much of New York!"

Pete grinned at her. "I know just how you feel. Jean and I are old New Yorkers. She's been here on trips and I've lived here almost a year. But we haven't calmed down about New York yet!"

The Fountain Room was another gorgeous surprise. Vicki heard the soft rush of water and, looking ahead into the spacious, stately room of white and blue, she discovered waterfalls cascading down trellises of fresh green foliage.

The headwaiter heard Vicki's gasp, as he led them under crystal chandeliers to the table which the boys had reserved.

"You admire our waterfalls, mademoiselle? They are true replicas of the water gardens for which the villas of Italy are famous," he told her.

A spotlighted orchestra in a band shell played a lilting tune. All twelve of Vicki's group were seated around one immense round table, gleaming with white damask and silver and crystal. Vicki looked eagerly at the people, talking and supping at adjoining tables, or dancing quietly on the small square of shining floor. She was fascinated by a black-haired woman all in black—by a snowy-haired man who looked as a king should look—by the absorbed pianist at the open grand piano—by the whole tinkling, softly sparkling room.

Waiters brought supper menus and they ordered. Bob recommended New York's typical sea-food dishes —lobster, crab, oyster, clam, shrimp—particularly for inlanders like Vicki and Jean and Bill Boyd, who were just discovering foods out of the Atlantic Ocean.

"New York!" Vicki said under her breath.

Bill Boyd at her left seconded that. Beyond him, Jean—still with Pete Carmody—was so thrilled that she gave the impression of bouncing in her chair. Smiling, Vicki looked around the circle of their vast table. Dot Crowley, seated between two of The Three Bears, was being very dignified. Celia chattered, but she was too far away for Vicki to hear what the southern girl was saying, over the dance music. Charmion, Vicki was glad to see, was talking and laughing with Bob, and seemed really to be enjoying herself. Vicki's gaze turned the full circle, coming to rest on Dean, at her right.

"Do you like it as much as I do, Dean?"

"Very nice. But I wouldn't want it every night in the week. Dance, Vicki?"

They excused themselves but it was unnecessary, for their whole table rose to dance.

Dancing with Dean in this beautiful room, to the music of a name band, Vicki reached the crest of her enjoyment.

"I'd rather dance than eat," she confessed.

"I'd rather fly than anything."

"Jean says she flew your Piper Cub."

"Tell you about my plane when we get back to the table."

Tessa and Bill Boyd danced alongside them. The boys exchanged partners, and Vicki found herself bumping along with Bill. He took enormous steps, turned mechanically, and Vicki suspected he was earnestly counting to himself. She was relieved when Bob cut in. Bob danced lightly and easily, and let the music do the talking.

When they returned to their table, the waiters had already brought in the casseroles of sea food. They all were served, and began to eat and talk. Vicki felt like talking, on this occasion, of cabbages or kings, of anything but their work. But Dean was eager to describe his Piper Cub to her.

It was a small plane, seating only two passengers, but it was sturdy, "and it can duck in and out of places where a larger ship can't go," Dean said. He explained that his four brothers felt they shared in the ownership of the plane, since they kept it clean for him, and his brother Bud occasionally flew it to some point where Dean wanted it.

"I usually keep the plane down in Charleston. Charleston, South Carolina—that's where my family lives," Dean told her. "But I'm starting on the Norfolk, Virginia, run, so I asked Bud to fly it up to Norfolk and leave it in the hangar for me. Maybe you and I can take a little spin around Norfolk, sometime."

"Nice, but when will I be in Norfolk?" Vicki said.

"Oh, maybe we can arrange it. It's not far from New York. Come on, let's dance some more."

She danced with Dean, and then with Don and Jerry. Only Pete did not ask her for a dance. But Pete was still sitting at their table with Jean when Vicki returned as the orchestra took an intermission. Pete and Jean were talking away together as if they were the only two people in this huge room.

"Well, well," Vicki thought. "They've discovered each other, after all these months! They certainly seem pleased about it!"

Vicki was pleased herself. She even felt a little relieved. Pete was likable, but Vicki had never been able to think of him as a potential romance. Now, Pete and Jean were a much happier combination, Vicki considered. Pete with his high jinks and tomboy Jean—yes, that made sense. Their delighted preference for each other this evening was pleasant to see, if comically obvious. Vicki hoped this might be the beginning of a real friendship.

"I like them both so much, I can quite understand what they see in each other!" she thought sympathetically. Charmion caught Vicki's eye across the table, and smiled toward the new Carmody-Cox twosome.

The waiters brought silver trays of pastries and silver pots of coffee. The room was quieter now, as the hour grew late. The girls looked at their watches with some concern. They had their careers to face tomorrow morning, and they needed sufficient sleep.

Leaving the Fountain Room, Pete suggested they take the girls home "the long way round. Let's take hansom cabs through Central Park. It's not too late for that!"

So they piled into taxis and drove up Fifth Avenue to Central Park Plaza. There they found three sleepy old men in rusty black tail coats and old silk hats, three mid-Victorian carriages, and three blanketed, ancient horses. They engaged all three hansoms, with two couples climbing up the high iron step into each one. Vicki and Dean, Jean and Pete, led off the moonlit parade of three frail, creaking carriages into the park.

Central Park was deserted and ghostly at night. Bare branches stretched out like arms and street lamps gleamed murkily along the curving driveways. None of them talked very much, in the swaying hansom. The horse's quick, sharp, even trot soothed Vicki and made her sleepy. She yawned in spite of herself.

"Excuse me!"

"I'm sleepy, too," Jean Cox admitted.

"You danced for hours," Dean defended them.

Pete stared out into the shadows. "I'll bet Bernard Shaw is hungry."

"Ohh-ahh—" Vicki yawned again and blinked hard, trying to keep awake. Thoughts of tomorrow morning's new run, and Jean and Pete's new romance, and ice skaters in white plumes, and waterfalls and crystal chandeliers, and Dean's Piper Cub all got mixed up in Vicki's head.

"Didn't we have a wonderful evening?" she murmured, and the hansom went rolling merrily on and on through the silent park.

CHAPTER III

New Assignment

IT WAS STIMULATING TO BE OUT AT THE AIRPORT THIS bright, blowing Monday morning. Here were bare fields, vast empty sky—and planes, roaring in or away. Vicki tingled in the cold wind and breathed in the smell of sea and gasoline. She hurried along to the airport buildings, excited at belonging to this powerful, far-flung web of aviation.

In the Stewardess Lounge, she signed in and picked up a letter from home. Then she headed for another building and the office of Assistant Superintendent of Flight Stewardesses Ruth Benson.

That sleek young woman, seated at a desk, was Vicki's adored boss. Miss Benson looked up at Vicki's knock and smiled at her out of brilliant gray eyes.

"Good morning, Miss Benson. I'm all ready for my new run!"

"And bursting with curiosity to know what it is?"

Vicki nodded and grinned. As Ruth Benson searched

among the papers on her desk, Vicki looked at her intently. Starting out as a flight stewardess herself, Ruth Benson had worked her way up to this executive post. She was a handsome young woman, assured poise in every move. She was only a few years older than Vicki, and Vicki openly admired her. She handed some papers across to Vicki.

"You're flying to Norfolk, Virginia. A nice run, Vicki. I hope you'll enjoy this route."

"Why—I—thank you, Miss Benson," Vicki stammered. Norfolk—then Dean was going to be her copilot. Nice! And he must have known all along that she was scheduled for this route. "Wait till I see that old tease!" she thought.

The papers indicated that Vicki was to fly out this morning, and that today's crew consisted of herself as stewardess, Dean Fletcher as copilot, and Captain Tom Jordan as pilot and commander of the plane. Vicki had flown before with Captain Jordan; she liked him very much.

"I'm sure I shall enjoy this assignment, Miss Benson."

"Good. And extra double good luck! Now you'd better hurry right over to the hangar."

Out in the cold again, Vicki thought about her new route. Ruth Benson seemed to consider it rather a choice one. But Vicki felt a little disappointed. It was such a short flight—no meals to serve aloft (for her flights were scheduled at 10:00 A.M. or 2:00 P.M., which were between-meals hours). No long distances to conquer, and thus no time to get to know the passengers. It sounded almost too brief and easy.

In the hangar, for the next forty minutes, Vicki went through the great gleaming plane in which she was to fly, and checked to see that everything was immaculate, in place, and the supplies complete. Captain Jordan sent her a copy of the manifest, the flight plan, and a weather report, which she studied in order to be able to answer her passengers' questions. Then, with a last tug at her trim blue jacket and skirt and cap, and a last peep in the mirror, Vicki went to find her crew.

She found Dean Fletcher standing right outside her plane, talking to a mechanic about the final tuning up. Dean looked dashing in his blue copilot's uniform, and completely unaware of it.

"Morning, Vicki. Surprised to see me? Mike, test that altimeter once more, will you?"

The pilot came up. Captain Jordan was a hearty, comfortable, dependable man, one of the nicest of the "big brother" pilots. Vicki was delighted to be assigned to him, and he in his turn thumped her on the shoulder.

"Look who's here! Our little yellow chick. It's cold this morning, Vicki. Put on your topcoat and button up."

The ground crew started wheeling the plane out of

the hangar, by small truck, and taxied it across the air-field. Vicki and the two fliers followed the plane. Out on one of the landing mats the crew chief directed the maneuvering of the ship into loading position. Vicki listened to the loading crew as they computed the weights of passengers, of mail and cargo, and of the gasoline load, so that they would take up only a safe weight. It was technical, and she felt a small spurt of pride at her know-how.

There was a minute's lull between completing the loading and letting the waiting passengers come aboard. Vicki whispered to Dean:

"I love this work."

His cool eyes lit up. "Me, too, Vic. Well, we're off now."

"Happy landings."

They shook hands on it, comrades in work, eyes sparkling over the prospect of a brand-new run.

The rope holding back the small crowd was re-moved. Vicki took her post at the cabin doorway, and the passengers streamed up the portable gangplank, to stop briefly before her, one by one. She checked off each person on her manifest before letting him enter the plane, smiling at each one and trying to tally each one's name with his appearance.

"Mr. Adair . . . no hair, Adair . . . Mrs. Taylor, beige coat, obviously a good *tailor* . . . Miss Peg Gossett, and who could resist that smile! . . . Mr.

and Mrs. O'Brien. He's the handsomest man I ever saw . . . Mr. Putnam. Hmm, Mr. Important. Mr. Fussy. Put-put-put-Putnam." Vicki took a few steps down the gangplank, and gave her hand and words of encouragement to a very old man. "Grandpa Marks. Have to look out for the old fellow. Marks. Age marks the spot . . . Mrs. Jensen and her baby, the cutie. Jensen, Jensen . . . Mr. Creel . . . Mr. Daniels . . . Mr. Cort . . ." Her plane was filling up.

The passengers took seats. The lighted sign was already on: FASTEN YOUR SAFETY BELT. NO SMOKING. Vicki went up and down the aisle to see that everyone was strapped in for the take-off. She also passed out chewing gum, explaining that frequent swallowing helps relieve pressure on eardrums, aloft. She gave a quick look at the heater, the ventilator, and ducking out the door, took from the passenger agent the pilot's logbook and the last batch of mail. All set! The cabin door was slammed shut and locked. Vicki went to the jump seat at the back of the cabin, and strapped herself in.

Now came the plane engine's deep-throated roar, as Captain Jordan and Dean started to warm up the great silver ship. The plane shook. Now another engine turned over, and roared. The propellers revolved, faster and faster, until they were whirling and invisible. The ground crew backed away. Clouds of dust arose. The starter's arm dropped.

The plane trembled like a live thing, and suddenly they rolled down the runway, gathering speed. Sensitively the wheels parted from the ground and the plane rose, soaring gradually at first, swaying, then climbing steadily and powerfully into the sky.

Vicki let out her breath. Every take-off was to her a miracle. The controlled, stored-up power, the tension, then the release—and breaking free from earth itself! Men in caves must have looked enviously on birds, and dreamed of flying. Men for centuries had retold the legends of Pegasus and Icarus, and had died in vain attempts to float in the air. Now here was this giant ten-ton ship, loaded with people, traveling along through the clouds—the dream come true.

But this was no time for daydreaming. Vicki wriggled out of her safety belt, and went about her business of seeing that the passengers were comfortable.

The Jensen infant was not sure it approved of flying. It hiccoughed in a surprised way, stared at the bright silver wing outside in the clouds and sun, started half-heartedly to wail, and decided against it.

"Mrs. Jensen," Vicki said over the plane's noise, leaning over her, "you needn't hold the baby in your arms, unless you want to. You might be more comfortable with the baby on a pillow in your lap."

Apparently that was a good arrangement, for Miss or Master Infant—Vicki could not tell which—immediately went to sleep and slumbered, nonstop as the plane itself, over New York, New Jersey, and Pennsylvania.

Most of the passengers settled down to looking out at the sky scenery, or reading newspapers, or napping. But Mr. Putnam buzzed crankily for the stewardess. Vicki came swaying unsteadily up the aisle, hanging on tight when the plane rolled once.

"Where's breakfast, young woman?" Mr. Putnam demanded.

"No meals are served on this ten A.M. flight, Mr. Putnam. But if you are hungry, I can give you a snack if you like."

She brought him bread and butter and cheese and fruit. Mr. Putnam gobbled it down. Vicki saw old Mr. Marks looking on wistfully, as if he would like some, too.

She stopped beside the old man's chair.

"Would you like a snack, Mr. Marks?" He cupped his ear. She bent over him and shouted: "Are you hungry?"

"Sure am."

"I'll bring you a lunch box—" and she also undid his seat belt, since the riding was smooth. Back with the snack, Vicki chatted with the old man.

"I see on my list that you're from Peoria, Mr. Marks. Do you miss Peoria?"

"Sure do."

"It must be a pretty lively town."

"Sure is."

Vicki sighed. This was a single-track conversation. "Well, enjoy your snack."

"Sure will."

"Ring this buzzer, here, if you want anything."

"Sure."

She left Mr. Marks chewing away, perfectly contented. And then he, like the baby, fell asleep.

The brief flight passed pleasantly and peacefully. Vicki, with little to do, had a chance to note the changing terrain below them. New York had been bare and cold but over Maryland and here in Virginia, even in November, still were patches of green, milder winds, and a bluer Atlantic.

Norfolk was as picturesque as Vicki hoped it might be. With several hours off before the return to New York, Dean offered to show her around the old seaport town. From the air she had seen its fifty miles of water front on Hampton Roads along Chesapeake Bay, and had had an aerial glimpse of the famous Navy Yard on the Portsmouth side, and the harbor thronged with trading ships of all nations.

"This is a great port," Dean told her. "So is my home town of Charleston. The South ships its products— cotton, tobacco, lumber, coal—all over the world from these two ports."

"But where do people live?" Vicki asked.

At the airport Dean secured a car, and the tall flier and his small assistant set out to see Norfolk.

First stop was noon lunch in the downtown section,

built up but still with the narrow streets of colonial days. Then they saw stately ante-bellum homes, with chrysanthemums and late roses in bloom in their gardens, and tall evergreens, drooping and sweeping like a lady's skirt. They drove past relics of the Civil War, and St. Paul's Church with a British cannon ball from Revolutionary days embedded in its walls; past open-air flower stands, and southern Quakers or Dunkards in their flat hats selling homemade sausage and scrapple from covered country wagons.

"This is the way I like to learn geography and history," Vicki remarked. "Painlessly—by travel."

Twenty miles east of Norfolk they found sailboats scudding along in the blue bay. Widely spaced houses stood between beach and pine woods. Dean parked the car near someone's big home, one which particularly appealed to Vicki. It was stained brown—of Douglas fir from Oregon, Dean said—with sparkling white trim; and from the profusion of richly draped windows looking out over water and woods, from the rambling spaciousness of the house, and the dooryard planted with brilliant yellow-green rye, one knew the family there lived well and loved the place. A young girl came out of the house and ran along the beach, running out of sight, as Vicki and Dean watched.

"Beautiful," sighed Vicki.

"Makes me homesick," Dean admitted suddenly. "We have chrysanthemums, and carmine and white roses, blooming at home in our garden at Charleston, right this minute. Doggone it, I'm going to get home —maybe toward the end of this month. And you're coming with me, Vicki."

"Am I?" She blinked. "How are we going to manage—"

"We'll get home for Thanksgiving." Dean went on planning aloud, not hearing her. "That's it, Thanksgiving. I'll write Mother that I'm bringing you. And we'll hop down in my plane. Guess I told you Bud flew it up to Norfolk for me. Better go see if it's safe in the hangar—"

He let out the clutch so abruptly and the car bounded forward so fast that Vicki could only yell:

"Hey! I'm falling out! And I didn't say I was coming!"

"—and we'll have turkey with corn-bread stuffing, bet you never tasted that—and scalloped oysters—"

"But I have to consult my own parents first!"

"Well, consult 'em. And you'll meet my four brothers—"

So it was all settled that Vicki and Dean were to fly to Charleston, come Thanksgiving Day.

CHAPTER IV

Southward Bound

THE DAY BEFORE THANKSGIVING FINALLY ARRIVED. FOR-
tunately their work schedule landed Vicki and Dean
in Norfolk, with adequate time off. At the airport they
scrambled out of uniform and into warm sports clothes,
said good-bye to Captain Tom Jordan, and raced for
the hangar where Dean's plane stood waiting—"so
tuned up she's ready to take off all by herself," Dean
said.

It was a bright red, scratched-up Piper Cub, so tiny
and fragile looking beside the commercial liners that
it seemed like a toy. The long-legged Dean could almost have picked it up and tucked it under his arm.
Vicki gulped. The name "Marietta" was painted on its
pointed nose with its toy-size propeller.

"Who's Marietta?"

"My mother."

"That's nice." But still Vicki hesitated. "Can we both
go up in that—that little teacup?"

"Why not?" Dean was indignant.

"Where'll I put my knees?" Vicki faltered.

"If I can fit in, you can. Just fold yourself up, like this"—Dean made a sort of jacknife of himself—"and crawl in. Like me." He turned on the ignition and grumbled under his breath, something about females.

Vicki's dander rose. She defiantly crawled into the glass-enclosed cubicle, slid down into the slippery leather seat, and glared at the back of Dean's head.

"Here." He reached around and strapped her in. "What's the matter—don't you think I know how to fly? Suppose you'll want a parachute, next."

Vicki's lower lip trembled. "Have you got a parachute—please? And stop being mad at me!"

The disgust on Dean's face gave way to amusement, and then gentled. "Look, honey. I like you. I'm taking you home with me because I think you're—swell. Well, then, I wouldn't take you up in just any old crate. Marietta is as reliable as I am. Now, you settle back and I'll explain what you'll see. Make a regular Cook's Tour out of this!"

The single little propeller spun, the little ship wobbled, and its motor shrilled like a mosquito. They went bumping down the airfield, Vicki's knees under her chin as if she were riding in a baby carriage. She was really astonished when she saw the ground slide away, and treetops recede under them.

Once up, the wind bounced them around like a

rubber ball, at first. But Dean got up speed and the riding became smooth. In fact, Vicki experienced a new freedom and lightness and agility, in the little plane, impossible in the heavy liners. The Piper Cub dipped, rose, spun, as carefree as a butterfly.

As they flew along, the scenery below them changed. Dean deliberately flew low, so that Vicki could enjoy the rolling hills and rivers of Virginia. They soon crossed the state line into North Carolina, and here the land became flat and sandy. Dean followed a winding river as landmark. Now the plane chugged steadily over a wooded valley. The Piper Cub's shadow on the trees below tagged after them.

"What a lot of trees!" Vicki called to Dean. "I thought the South was all cotton fields."

"Oh, no," he said over his shoulder. "Plenty of cotton, of course, and tobacco. But the Carolinas have tremendous timber tracts. Look down. See that bare space in the woods? That's where they've been logged out."

Vicki looked down and began to watch, rather than merely admire. Dean pointed out a virgin forest; then a tract that had been partly cut over; then another spot where only tree stumps remained, and new, young trees were growing.

"Logging's a big business," he called. "Look—down to your right, at the edge of the river. We're going right over a lumber mill—those big sheds. See it? See those enormous logs? Yes, there's a fortune growing all through here."

Vicki thought of all the things lumber is used for: houses, factories, schools, ships, railroad ties, fuel, paper pulp, and by-products like turpentine, tar, medicines. Dean told her the United States is the largest lumber-producing country in the world, and trees from these peaceful forests are shipped all over the world.

"From these forests by railroad to the seaports. Then abroad. From Norfolk to Great Britain. From Charleston to South America."

He pointed the plane's nose down and they dropped until they were barely skimming the tops of trees. He taught Vicki to understand what she was looking at: valuable stands of cypress; valuable and magnificent hickory; second-growth ash, valuable too; and the lesser gum, black gum, oak, and low-grade pine. Dean explained that not much of the valuable timbers were left in North Carolina. Only a few, long-owned, family tracts still stood uncut.

Once a plane passed them, and Vicki wanted to know what it was.

"A forest ranger on patrol. He's out to spot and prevent forest fires. I guess you know what fire in these woods could do!"

And Dean pointed out a fire tower, high on a hill overlooking the forests. Vicki listened, breathed in the smell of pine and swamp. The air grew softer still as the Piper Cub flew steadily south. Dean doggedly talked lumbering. By the time they came down at the Charleston airport, Vicki felt as if her own head, as well as her cramped knees, were made of wood.

The drive from the airport to Dean's house took them through many lovely Charleston streets. Vicki realized she was in a large city, and a magnificent one. It still bore brilliant traces of its wealthy and cultured seventeenth and eighteenth century English settlers. Here were colonial homes with pillared porticoes and spacious verandas, great estates, famous old gardens with live oaks, palmettos, and camellias, glimpsed through wrought-iron gates. In the twilight, Charleston seemed enchanted.

The Fletcher house was not a grand old one, but hospitable and comfortable. It showed the marks of a predominantly masculine family: a sailboat rudder propped in the entrance hall; pipes in the ash trays; a leather jacket flung on a chair.

Dean's cool eyes, clean-boned face, and absorbed air he had inherited, obviously, from his mother. But Mrs. Fletcher was small and plump and dainty, and her hair was graying. She welcomed Vicki warmly.

"You can't imagine how pleased we are to have a young lady staying with us, Miss Barr—very well then, Vicki. You'll be a good influence on my houseful of boys! Every one of them is so eager to meet you."

Dean's father came in, took the pipe out of his mouth to speak a brief welcome, and excused himself. Since he was a bit taciturn and an engineer, and since Vicki, after repeatedly failing mathematics in school, stood in awe of all engineers, she decided not to concentrate on Mr. Fletcher.

However, Dean's four younger brothers promised a lively stay here. Howdy and Chips burst in first. They were freshly scrubbed, damply combed, excited about having a visitor.

Howdy was six, with a tooth out in front. He acclaimed Vicki as "the purtiest lady I ever saw. Besides, we got the same color hair!" he noticed happily.

"That's a bond between us," Vicki agreed.

Chips was ten, very gruff in his effort to act grown up. He shook hands with Vicki in a complicated grip —his Boy Scout troop's special, secret grip, he explained, and said, "Glad to have you aboard."

"Susie made pecan pie," Howdy hissed through the gap in his teeth. "Want to see my dog Duke?"

"We have pecan pie when company comes," Chips stated hoarsely. "That's why I'm glad you came."

"Chips!" Dean was mortified. But Mrs. Fletcher merely smiled, and excused herself.

A boy of twelve marched in. He was Alan, grave like Dean. "Pleased to meet you," and he said no more.

"Can you wrestle, Vicki?" Howdy asked.

"Can you do parachute jumps?" Chips croaked.

"No, but I'm going to play cops and robbers with you—if you'll play with an old lady like me."

"You aren't so old," Alan said suddenly.

"I'm forty-five."

Alan smiled faintly, but Chips and Howdy studied her. Chips at last shook his head. Howdy in the meantime had forgotten what the question was.

A tall gangling boy of seventeen was the last to come in, the brother who had flown the Piper Cub up to Norfolk. He and Dean exchanged smiles.

"Vicki, this is my brother Cornelius—Bud."

The boy blushed furiously and pushed out an oversize hand. "With a name like Cornelius, you see why they call me Bud."

Vicki smiled back. "I suppose if you'd been christened Bud, they'd call you Cornelius."

Bud chuckled. "Would you like to see the garden?"

"And meet Duke!" Howdy reminded her.

Vicki, knee-deep in small boys, inspected a nondescript, long-tailed, extremely friendly dog, the doghouse in the back yard, the garden, and Howdy's "secret hiding place for messages" in the grape arbor. All the brothers, including Dean, were anxious to have Vicki see and approve everything. She barely had a moment to make herself presentable for dinner.

Dinner went pleasantly. There were black-eyed peas and hominy, typically southern, along with the rest of the meal. Vicki was a little confused by the

activity five boys can create at table, even with a pair
of parents in charge. Alan tossed Dean a roll, the full
length of the table, before his father could reprimand
him. Chips tied his napkin over his head and made
faces. Howdy spilled most of a jar of piccalilli onto his
plate, and protested sadly when the fruits of his accident were taken away from him. Vicki tried to devote
herself to her hostess. But with five boys demanding,
one after another, "another glass of milk, please,
Mother," Mrs. Fletcher's conversation was absent-
minded.

"Have you a brother?" she asked Vicki, in a lull.

"No, Mrs. Fletcher, a sister but no brothers."

"You must have a peaceful household," Mrs. Fletcher
commented.

Not long after dinner, Howdy was torn away by
main force from Vicki's side, and sent upstairs to bed.
Alan, who was frankly bored with girls, and Chips
settled down to do their homework. None of the three
were happy with these arrangements, but Mrs. Fletcher
consoled them with a reminder that tomorrow was
Thanksgiving.

Bud and Vicki and Dean decided to go out in Bud's
jalopy. Chips at his books called after them: "I wish
I was grown up already, too!"

The jalopy was falling apart, but it ran. They went
clanking downtown in it, and stopped at Bud's favorite
shop to drink cokes and listen to the juke box. They

did not stay long, for Vicki wanted a chance to visit with her hosts.

Next morning they all went to church for Thanksgiving services. The music was unusually fine, and the church a beautiful old one, with sun shining gloriously through stained-glass windows. Vicki, sitting with the Fletchers in their pew, listened to the Reverend Mr. Martin retell the stirring story of Thanksgiving.

At the church door, after the service, Vicki was introduced to the minister. Mr. Martin had a twinkle in his eye.

"How is your dog Duke?" he said to Howdy. "I hear he came to Sunday school with you last Sunday."

Howdy was overcome with shyness by this notice of his pet. But the moment the Reverend Mr. Martin turned to other members of his congregation, Howdy's tongue became unloosed and wagged all the way home.

"It was *nice* with Dukey under my chair. He didn't bark a-tall, only when Teacher passed out the psalm card, he crawled out an' chewed up Mary Webster's, an' she cried, an' Teacher put Duke out an' said: 'Shoo! Go home!' an' Teacher said Duke smelled."

"Better not take Duke again," his mother said gently. "We all have a very good idea of what happened!"

The turkey was not quite done, Susie announced. Vicki and the five boys filled in the time playing a watered-down version of baseball in the back yard.

The brothers admitted Vicki could run, but said unkind things about her batting. They put her on second base, which was Duke's doghouse, and Vicki felt it was symbolic.

Thanksgiving Day dinner at the Fletchers' was a real feast. Afterwards Vicki and the boys were too full and lazy to do anything but sit on the porch steps. Amid the silence and yawns, Vicki made a great effort.

"Does anyone present like limericks?"

"What's that?" chorused Howdy and Chips.

"Well, here's one, for example," and Vicki recited:

> *"An epicure dining at Crewe,*
> *Found quite a large mouse in his stew.*
> *Said the waiter, 'Don't shout,*
> *And wave it about,*
> *Or the rest will be wanting some, too!' "*

They approved. Chips responded with "The Purple Cow." Bud said he had learned a new one, "if I can twist my tongue around it." And he declaimed:

> *"There was a young lady of Woosester,*
> *Who usest to crow like a roosester,*
> *She usest to climb*
> *Two trees at a time,*
> *But her sisester usest to boosest her."*

Alan came out of his detachment to repeat, wryly, this jingle:

"There was a young man from Japan,
Who wrote verses no one could scan.
When they told him 'twas so,
He said, 'Yes, I know,
But I try to get as many words in the last
line as I can.' "

They declared that was the limerick to end all
limericks. Howdy wandered off with the dog. Chips
and Alan got out the checkerboard and started a game.
The "old ones" chatted, and time pleasantly drifted
by.

Suddenly Dean looked at his watch and exclaimed:
"Whoops, Vicki, do you realize what time it is?
We'd better get along. We've got to get to Norfolk
before dark, because my Piper isn't equipped for night
flying."

They ran. Vicki threw her few things into her overnight bag. With Dean, she hunted up the parents,
Susie, and the boys. Vicki was sorry to say good-bye,
for she had enjoyed herself in the Fletchers' house.

"You'll be coming back soon again, I hope, Vicki,"
Mrs. Fletcher said. "In fact, I'm going to insist on it."

"I'd love to, Mrs. Fletcher, and thank you for a
wonderful Thanksgiving. Good-bye. 'Bye, fellows."
Vicki stopped to hug Howdy, and pat Duke's lop ears.

Then she and Dean ran to the jalopy, where Bud
sat waiting to drive them back to the Charleston airport—back on their way to work.

CHAPTER V

Vicki Finds Joan

ON VICKI'S RETURN FLIGHT FROM NORFOLK TO NEW YORK, a pleasant crowd of people filled the sunny cabin. Those pillars of strength, Captain Tom Jordan and Copilot Dean, were up in front in the pilots' cabin. Vicki went about her duties on the gently rocking plane, and felt warmly satisfied to be back at work in the sky.

She tilted a chair back for a passenger, helped a man read an air map, brought a blanket for a woman who had been ill. Then Vicki looked again at the young girl in Seat 8.

She was about nineteen, poised, quiet, nicely dressed. But her face held such woe that Vicki's curiosity had been aroused. More than curiosity—concern. Joan Purnell, the manifest said. The only other thing Vicki knew about her was that she was traveling alone.

Her very light-blonde eyebrows made her appear blonder and younger than she was, and gave her a candid look. The fine straight gold-brown hair, caught by a velvet band and falling simply around her face, was deceptively childish, too. But in the level eyes shone intelligence. Vicki was sorry to see such an obviously nice girl sitting like a statue of grief.

Vicki went on studying her and speculating about her. Her black suit was probably the most grown-up garment the girl possessed, Vicki decided. She wondered why Joan Purnell carried no luggage. Was she merely going to New York for the day? But this was the 2:00 P.M. plane which would get her into New York rather late in the day. Unless she turned right around and flew back, she would almost have to stay overnight in New York. Odd. A business person might make a hasty trip without luggage, leaving in a hurry. But this girl clearly lived with her family, and looked like a student. Yes, it was odd.

Vicki's curiosity was not idle. As stewardess in charge of the passenger cabin, the welfare of the passengers was her responsibility. Bewilderment, illness, trouble—it was up to Vicki to assist with these.

She tried speaking to Joan Purnell.

"Wouldn't you like a magazine?"

"No, thank you." The girl's voice was muffled.

"Or a snack?"

"Nothing, thanks—well, yes, I would like something to eat. I left without having lunch."

So she left in a hurry, Vicki thought. Or perhaps she was too upset to eat.

Vicki brought the girl a lunch box and left her. She might feel more cheerful and communicative with some food in her.

But after Joan Purnell had finished, and Vicki came along the aisle to relieve her of the box and waxed paper, all the girl said was, "Thank you very much." She gripped her hands together and turned her face to the plane window.

Vicki said kindly, "Isn't there anything else I can do for you?"

"I—nothing, thank you," the girl said in a very low tone of voice. She seemed uncomfortable under Vicki's forget-me-not blue eyes, so Vicki tactfully started to move off.

But then the girl opened a purse well filled with bills. "I forgot to pay you for the lunch," she said.

"There is no charge for meals aloft on Federal Airlines, Miss Purnell."

So the girl was not used to flying, was not used to casually catching a plane—without luggage. The contents of her purse spelled no lack of means or indulgent family protection.

Joan Purnell nervously closed her purse. She eyed Vicki and tried to compose herself.

"Your first flight?" Vicki said conversationally.

"You've certainly picked a beautiful clear day for it."

"Yes."

"I haven't been flying long myself. Do you like it?"

"Oh—Yes. Yes, I like flying very much."

"You seemed rather tense," Vicki said carefully. "I thought perhaps you weren't enjoying the trip."

Joan Purnell's velvety eyes shot Vicki a look of resentment. "I'm enjoying it very much." She stared dully at her hands.

"If something's wrong," Vicki persisted gently, "won't you tell me? Won't you let me try to help you?"

Joan's youthful face suddenly relaxed, as if she was about to cry. Vicki thought that here was a sensitive and vulnerable girl indeed, who would be liable to take things hard. Joan's lips quivered, but she firmly kept her silence.

Another passenger buzzed Vicki, and once more she left Joan Purnell. The flight was more than half over. Vicki hoped she could win the girl's confidence before the plane landed in New York, and this overwrought girl was swallowed up in the crowds of the city. Of course, once Joan Purnell was off the plane, Vicki's responsibility technically ended. But Vicki's sympathies were not bounded by the rules of her job. That girl was in trouble and needed help!

"I've seen her before," Vicki mused. "I know I have. Somewhere. Where was it? Recently, too."

She reviewed faces, scenes, dates. But hundreds of

faces passed before her, on the planes, at the airports, in various cities. Joan's face remained bafflingly un-identified. Even the name roused no echoes in Vicki's memory.

On her way back from the pilots' cabin, Vicki found Joan crying. She sat erect and wept with a terrible, stony quiet.

Vicki sat down on the arm of her chair, shielding her from the gaze of the other passengers.

"Come, now," Vicki murmured. "Don't cry. Don't turn away from me. I'm just another girl like yourself. Can't you talk to me?"

Joan Purnell took a deep, quivering breath and wiped the tears off her round cheeks.

"I can't stand it any more. I've tried and tried— But no more." She cried out passionately, "No more!"

"You're running away," Vicki guessed.

Joan nodded miserably. Her hair swung and almost hid her face.

Vicki said gently, "You can't run away from troubles. You only take them with you to a new place."

"Well, maybe the new place will be better." The girl was talking wildly. "Maybe my aunt in New York will be more understanding than my mother."

Vicki smiled a little. "Too much family life? That's understandable."

Joan lifted her eyes. Wan humor lurked there. "You really do understand?"

"How does running away solve anything?"

Joan considered. "It doesn't," she admitted. "I suppose it's cowardly to run away. But Mother, even Dad, makes things so difficult— Though in a way, it's only because everything is going wrong at home. I don't understand what's happening."

Then with a rush the girl exclaimed, "And I'm not really running away! I'm going to visit my aunt Sue. I used to spend my holidays with her when I was a little girl. From childhood she always seemed to know how I felt about things. So when things began to get so—so hectic and miserable at home I wanted to be with Aunt Sue. She'll understand. She always has."

Vicki shook her fair head. "Family troubles, and the repercussions are hurting you?"

"Something like that. Mother acts so strangely, and Dad isn't himself these days." She looked at Vicki in woebegone appeal. "I suppose you think that because I'm running away I don't care for them. But I do, I love them very much. That's exactly why all this hurts so much."

Vicki wondered what was causing the unhappiness in the Purnell home. She did not like to ask. She did permit herself to say, out of a desire to help Joan:

"Can't you get to the root of the unhappiness—the cause—and deal with it?"

Joan said a surprising thing. "I'm not sure I know

what the real cause is. Dad doesn't tell us very much. But I know he is terribly worried."

So some mysterious outside force had caught the entire Purnell family in its grip. It was hurting them so badly that it had driven Joan out of her own home. Vicki felt distressed, and much puzzled.

"You're awfully nice to talk to me like this, Miss V. Barr."

"The V. on the name plate is for Vicki."

The two girls smiled at each other. Joan Purnell seemed subdued but more calm now that she had talked over, and thought over, her difficulties.

"Please don't think I'm being childish or—or cow-ardly. But I suddenly felt that I just had to see Aunt Sue. I didn't let her know. Oh, I hope she will be there." She paused. Then she looked down at her clenched hands and said in a meek little voice, "But I guess you think I ought to be back home helping instead of adding to their worries."

Vicki tugged at a silvery blonde lock and reflected. "Those are just surface questions— Of course," she interrupted herself, "I think you ought to go home— not worry the life out of your parents—you say they're distracted enough as it is. Better send them a wire when we land. But the thing for you to do—the main thing —is to try to determine the cause of your family's un-happiness. And do something about it."

Joan smiled wanly, and a hint of the high spirits and affection latent in her glimmered through.

"I feel one hundred and fifty per cent better," she said earnestly. "You're right—I mustn't distress my parents any further. And I must look this problem in the eye. You think clearly, Miss V. Barr—Vicki, I mean."

Vicki grinned at her. It was a relief to see Joan getting a grip on herself, even if only temporarily. Yet the young stewardess had the feeling that the runaway was concealing from her the real cause of her family's trouble. Vicki still did not feel satisfied to turn Joan Purnell loose at the airport. Her worries might descend on her again, and drive her back into that black mood. Or suppose her aunt was out of town, and Joan was left wandering alone in a great city? The girl was not an experienced enough traveler for Vicki to be sure she would get home safely.

"See here, Joan," Vicki suggested. "Where does your aunt live?"

Joan Purnell told her the address.

"That's near where my apartment is. Suppose I go with you to your aunt's? Then, in case she isn't home, you can stay overnight with me." Vicki was too diplomatic to say what was really in her mind. She wanted personally to deliver Joan at her aunt's door, for that was the only way she could be sure the girl really would get there.

"You're very kind to befriend me. As a matter of fact," Joan confessed, "I haven't the slightest idea how to get to my aunt's. She's moved since the last time I visited her."

"Don't you worry," Vicki said, getting to her feet. Someone was signaling the stewardess. The FASTEN SEAT BELT sign had flashed on. "I'll take you to your aunt's this afternoon, and tomorrow I'll call for you and take you back to Norfolk on my run."

Joan obediently nodded. "I feel like Goldilocks being saved from the Three Bears."

"You mean Red Ridinghood—and I'm Grandma."

Vicki spoke lightly, but she thanked her lucky stars that she had caught Joan Purnell at the psychological moment. She only hoped that she would be able to help Joan, from this point on.

CHAPTER VI

Friends

"WHAT ARE YOU SO SERIOUS ABOUT?" CHARMION demanded of Vicki that evening.

"Yes, stop brooding and tell your dear old pals," Jean said.

The three girls were the only stewardesses in the apartment this cold autumn evening; Celia and Tessa and Dot were out on flights. Vicki's little trio—the original nucleus of their crowd—sat in the living room, having supper. Mrs. Duff had set up the small table in the window, and as they ate they looked out on the fabulous lights of New York. All three of them had been flying and were tired now, and relaxing. Charmion's long hair streamed over her shoulders, Jean wore pajamas, and Vicki had surrendered to stocking feet.

"Come on, Vicki, break down and tell us."

"I caught a runaway girl on my plane."

"Really! This afternoon?"

"That's plenty serious. Where is she?"

"Safe at her aunt's, about three blocks away. I took her there myself. And I'm going to take her back home to Norfolk myself," Vicki said.

"I should think so!" Charmion exclaimed. "These foolish children—"

"She's not a child, and she's not foolish," Vicki said slowly. "I think there's something very strange going on in her home—afflicting her entire family. I'm pretty sure that she knows more about what is behind the family trouble than she told me. And I think she feels ashamed now that she ran to her aunt instead of standing by her parents in their trouble, whatever it is."

Charmion and Jean demanded to hear the whole story.

"Well, don't you get mixed up in somebody else's family problem," Charmion warned.

"I may, whether I intend to or not." Vicki was thinking aloud. "Because I want to help Joan Purnell—I like that girl. Why, I couldn't simply set her down on her doorstep and then forget all about her! Uh—let's change the subject."

"Yes, let's," Charmion agreed. She grinned at Jean. "And how were your three dates with Peter Carmody?"

Jean Cox looked fussed. "How'd you find out?"

"Oho!" Vicki reached over and ruffled Jean's cropped hair. "Secret trysts, huh?"

"Secret with about ten million people around! We

met in the Fifth Avenue Library and spent the time sitting under one of the stone lions, out in front, talking and eating peanuts." She added apologetically that Pete's newspaper did not overpay him.

"Did Pete hold your hand?" Vicki teased.

"We also went to a fire," Jean said doggedly. "Followed the fire engines."

Charmion turned to Vicki. "We'll have to go to the library ourselves—and get Jean and Pete to read a book." Her gentle face was full of unselfish pleasure at Jean's good times. "As for me," the young widow confessed, "I had marriage proposals from two passengers this week."

"I'm not a bit surprised!"

"Someone nice?"

Charmion giggled. "One was bald and the other had false teeth. Not that," Charmion said hastily, "there aren't some darling people who are bald and have false teeth. But I—well—"

Vicki said quickly, "We know how it is. One's true love must be someone young and pretty—like Mickey Mouse."

It was a good sign that Charmion could laugh about the "love department."

Jean reported that little Celia Trimble was working hard at a special, speeded-up course in baby care, so eager was she to be assigned to the nursery plane. Tessa and Dot were deep in brand-new Spanish grammars. They insisted on saying *"gracias"* instead of "thank you," and *"sí"* instead of "yes" at every opportunity.

"What's up?" Vicki asked.

"Didn't you see the announcement? No, of course you couldn't have—it was posted while you were away. You don't know about the chance to go to Mexico!" Jean all but shrieked.

"You see, Vicki," Charmion explained, "Federal Airlines now has an affiliated airline in Mexico. The superintendent has just announced he is looking for two flight teams—maybe more later—and that means Miss Benson is looking for two stewardesses—to send down to Mexico around the first of the year."

"You mean"—Vicki was breathless—"two of us have a chance to fly in Mexico? Be sent to a foreign country? A *tropical* country?"

"Yes."

Vicki pretended to swoon. "I can speak Spanish," she said hopefully. "With a pure Castilian accent learned in Illinois."

"Do you speak it well?"

"It's fluent, if not always absolutely correct. I always liked Spanish, and it's so close to English and Latin that it just came natural."

"I speak fairly good French, but no Spanish," Charmion mourned.

Jean wrinkled her nose. "I know some Spanish and

German. I can only limp along in French." Vicki admitted her French would make a Frenchman gnash his teeth.

Vicki's eyes were very wide and blue. "Mexico. Mmmm!"

Charmion chuckled. "That's the way every single stewardess on Federal Airlines feels about it. It's a prize!"

Vicki dreamed that night of purple volcanoes, parrots, flower-spangled fiestas, and the bright, tropical Pacific. She awoke to frost and New York.

Early the next afternoon Vicki called for Joan.

With permission, she was taking Joan Purnell with her in the crew car, for the drive out to the airport. Dean was already in the crew car. Vicki had told him a little about Joan just before their northern flight had ended.

Vicki found a serious and thoughtful Joan waiting for her. Her face was pale and her level brown gaze was turned inward. She acknowledged the introduction to Copilot Fletcher without much interest and was silent on the drive to the airport. She sat quiet in the waiting room while Vicki went to the hangar to check up the plane, and Dean went off to the meteorologists' room for a wind and weather report.

It was a glorious afternoon, though Vicki nearly blew away, standing in the open cabin door as she checked her passengers aboard. They looked like an amiable group, choosing where they would sit. Vicki suggested to Joan that she take the seat at the back of the plane. It was bumpier riding back there, but it was next to the stewardess's jump seat and the girls would have a chance to talk. They took off at two o'clock, exactly on schedule, soaring up off the airstrip and past the glass control tower like a giant bird.

Today Vicki was less interested in her passengers— though passengers were the great adventure of flying, for her—than in the extraordinary sky the airship was smoothly roaring through. Never twice the same, never from minute to minute the same, today's sky was the clear acid blue of winter. Thin, sharp, translucent, the blue dazzled like diamonds and ice. The plane banked, lifted, turned on a steep angle. Vicki caught her breath at being whirled in the midst of this un-earthly beauty. "Formerly reserved for angels only," she thought.

The passengers did not require anything of the stewardess beyond routine attentions. Vicki conscientiously took care of her planeful, reported to the two pilots, and then sank down in the seat beside Joan's.

"Feeling more cheerful today?"

Joan looked anything but cheerful, hunched in her black suit, expression sober.

"When I think of going back, and facing it all over again—well, no, I don't feel particularly cheerful." She faced Vicki. Determination stiffened her bearing.

"But I feel more realistic than I did yesterday, at least!"

Vicki nodded and held her tongue.

Joan went on: "You know, when I faced my aunt, I felt like an awful ninny. And then I got to thinking about the way I'd weakly let you influence me, and I was pretty mad at you."

"At me?" Vicki said, alarmed.

Joan giggled. "Oh, I got over that foolish idea right away. Vicki—" and her candid gaze under the very fair brows appealed to Vicki—"you've helped me a lot, and I wish you'd help me some more."

"If I can. I want to help you, Joan. In what way do you mean?"

"Well, I want to come to grips with this problem. As you said, find out what's causing all the nerves and bad tempers and worry in my house. You think straight, Vicki. Help me think this out."

Vicki asked if Joan actually did not know what the cause was. Joan hesitated, and then began a curious story. The girl was vague, but this time she was honestly telling as much as she knew.

Joan's father, who was a scholar and not a business-man, was dreadfully worried about something. Joan suspected that his worry was what made her mother so irritable, too.

"Mother is a rather fluttery person, anyway. She's sweet, but she's always been badly spoiled because she's so beautiful. And that's made her dependent on other people. She doesn't know how to deal with a wrong order from the grocery, much less a big situation like what's worrying poor Dad. She depends on Dad for everything, even to order dinner—she's like a child, you see. And now that Dad is so busy with this business, and has no time for her, Mother has gone to pieces. So irritable, too!" Joan said emotionally.

"Don't blame your mother," Vicki pointed out. "Blame the root cause behind her display of nerves."

"Yes. That's right."

Joan then gave Vicki a confused account of a distant lumber business in which her father was involved. He had a partner, working somewhere in the timber tracts. Joan did not know much about the partner. She spoke hesitantly, fumbling for facts. Finally she blurted out:

"All I'm sure of is this—we're going broke. Fast. And Dad can't put his finger on the reason why. We might even lose our home."

Vicki turned over in her mind the fragments of information Joan had narrated. There simply were not enough pieces to put together to yield a coherent, meaningful whole. If that was all the scholarly Mr. Purnell knew about his business interests, as Joan insisted, Vicki thought wryly that he had better make a full and rapid investigation. Joan was busy with thoughts of her own, and her face had turned dreamy. Presently she said shyly:

"I'd like to show you a snapshot of my boat."

She drew from her purse a small leather folder and handed it across the aisle to Vicki. Vicki found a snapshot of Joan and two boys aboard a small catboat, smiling and squinting in the sun. Vicki looked closely at Joan in the picture. She wore dungarees and sweater, her straight fine hair was blowing, her face was smudged and happy.

"So that is Joan when she is herself," Vicki thought. She handed back the case, saying, "I've never been sailing on anything but lakes and rivers. You go out in the Atlantic in that little boat? Mm!"

"You come sail with me! This spring!" Joan said eagerly. "You'll come for a long week end and stay at our house—" She checked herself. "That is, if we still have our house by spring."

"Surely your father will get this business problem settled," Vicki said.

Joan slowly shook her head. "I'm not so sure."

Vicki felt very sorry indeed.

The girls talked on, Vicki rising from time to time and going to her passengers. Joan had nothing to add to her meager facts about her father's lumber business.

As the plane neared Norfolk, Joan grew more and more subdued. Vicki had no time to give her at the landing. "Wait for me," Vicki insisted. She was afraid that now, at the last minute, the troubled girl might slip away. And Vicki had to get her passengers off the plane, check over the ship for any lost articles, turn in her reports, explain to Dean and Captain Jordan that she was taking Joan home, instead of going to the Norfolk hotel where their crew was scheduled to stay.

Joan Purnell waited for her. She seemed small and scared as Vicki hurried up to her in the airport waiting room.

"I didn't even stop to change out of flight uniform," Vicki said breathlessly. "Sorry to keep you waiting. One of my passengers stopped me to tell me what a nice dear sweet hostess I am. As if I didn't know." Vicki put her tongue in her cheek.

"I'll wait," Joan said. "I'll wait for you as long as necessary. Because you've got to help me through this."

"Here, here, don't look so grim! Come on, we'll have a soda before we start out. A big fat chocolate soda. Do you know there's enough energy stuff in a chocolate soda to send us out to dig a ditch?"

"I don't want to dig a ditch."

"I know, I know. All right, I'll stop being gay and hollow for your sake. I'll be grim, too." Vicki scowled and held it. "How's that? Better?"

Joan was past response. She told Vicki where she lived: outside Norfolk proper, near Virginia Beach on Linkhorn Bay. The two girls set out in a taxi. It was rather a long and difficult route.

Coming to ocean and beach and pine woods, Vicki thought it looked familiar. This was the road where

Dean had driven her. She remembered the tall drooping evergreens, the carpet of pine needles, the crimson branch of dogwood, although no flowers or leaves were left now. Some of the houses looked familiar, too.

They drove up to a rambling, brown house with white doors and windows. Its dooryard was still yellow-green with late rye.

"Oh, yes," Vicki murmured. "That's the house I particularly admired."

"Did you? That's good, because I live here," Joan said.

Vicki was thinking: That's where I've seen Joan before. She came out of this house and went running along the beach. Strange, that I should have had a preview of her.

They paused at the tall hedge. "And this is where you're going to stay tonight," Joan added.

Vicki roused herself. "No, Joan, I can't barge in on your family unannounced. Thank you anyway."

"But I'd love to have you stay. Besides, please help me explain to my parents about running away—they'll feel much more satisfied if they meet you," Joan pleaded.

Vicki tried to decline. She would have liked to visit in this big, inviting house. But the Purnells were not expecting her, and at a troubled time like this they might not want a house guest, particularly a stranger.

"No, Vicki, not 'another time,'" Joan said huskily. "You promised to help me think this through. But more than the promise—we're friends, aren't we?"

Vicki's smile started from deep inside, and lit up her small face and compassionate eyes.

"Yes, Joan, we're friends."

Running out to the roadside, she paid and dismissed the taxi driver. A moment later she was following Joan through the dooryard. Joan Purnell lifted the brass eagle knocker, opened the white door, and Vicki stepped through.

CHAPTER VII

The Crumpled Note

"JOAN! THANK HEAVENS, YOU'RE HOME!"

A small man of about fifty came hurrying and limping into the entrance hall. Mr. Purnell embraced his daughter, and Joan hugged him.

"Yes, I'm all right, Dad! Dad, this is Miss Victoria Barr."

"You're in flight uniform—" He guessed instantly. "You must have found Joan? Miss Barr, I'm so grateful to you. So happy to have you here."

"Yes, Dad, Vicki came to the rescue." Joan told the story.

Joan's father shook Vicki's hand warmly with almost pathetic gratitude. Mr. Purnell was an appealing person, small in bone and stature, with a scholar's stooped shoulders, fine hands and delicate features. He was dressed in a soft, shabby tweed suit—tobacco brown, matching his thin fringe of hair and his warm, reflective eyes like Joan's eyes.

72

"Miss Barr—Victoria—you must be our guest, for as long as you are able, and every time you pass through Norfolk," Mr. Purnell said.

"Thank you, Mr. Purnell." Vicki was beginning to feel embarrassed. "Sometime when it is more convenient for you—"

"It is always convenient. You have done us a very great service, and Mrs. Purnell and I—"

A lady in a fluttery pink negligee came tripping down the staircase.

"Joan! My darling! How could you have done this terrible thing? You've prostrated me!"

"Now, Mother," said Joan.

"Now, Arabella," said Mr. Purnell.

Vicki had a hasty look at Joan's mother, as she wiped tears from her eyes. It was clear that Mrs. Purnell had once been a great beauty. Rather faded and fussy now, she retained all the airs of the belle she had once been.

Joan introduced Vicki to her. Mrs. Purnell held out a very white, soft hand.

"I can never thank you enough, my dear. You're sweet to deliver Joan to the very door. But you look such a child yourself. So—so helpless looking!"

Vicki squirmed. Joan noticed and tried not to grin.

Mr. Purnell said, "Quiet manner, bold spirit, Arabella." His eyes twinkled, and Vicki wondered if he was not also describing himself.

"Carter, this is no time to joke," his wife protested. "When our poor little Joan—"

"Joan is quite all right, and instead of fussing over her, we ought to give her a spanking," Mr. Purnell said genially. "Let's go into the sitting room, shall we? Victoria has had quite a responsibility with our daughter; perhaps she would like a glass of sherry, or some tea."

Limping, he led the way into a room paneled in knotty pine and furnished in chintzes. A fire burned slowly in the fireplace. Portraits and bird prints hung on the walls. Mrs. Purnell, behaving more like a guest than the hostess, swished along after them, her long negligee trailing on the polished floor.

Mr. Purnell drew the two girls down on either side of him on the couch. Joan's mother arranged herself in the fan chair, under the portrait of herself. They talked for a while of Joan's escapade. Mrs. Purnell warmly renewed their invitation to Vicki. Tea was brought in. The conversation went on, polite, aimless. Vicki sensed a tension here, under the hospitality and the gracious manners.

"It must be a strain for them," she thought, "to sit here and make conversation, and try to conceal their unhappy state of mind. I'll excuse myself."

She telephoned the pilot that she would be staying overnight with the Purnells. Then Joan took Vicki upstairs to the room that was to be hers—and every time she came, Mrs. Purnell assured her. It was a delightful room, with wall covering, draperies, and bedspread of mulberry and white, in the *toile* design—tiny shepherdesses and their sheep, trees blowing, a summer's day printed forever on cotton. Joan showed Vicki the curious old powder table, which opened. Then she took Vicki to the window and showed her the inlet dotted with boats.

"It's so lovely here, I wish I could stay forever," Vicki sighed.

"Now you know how I'd feel about losing this place." Joan linked her arm through Vicki's. "After dinner, let's talk to Dad about the lumber business."

Vicki said, "Your father will be much obliged to have a girl he barely knows prying into his business affairs."

"You don't know Dad. He won't feel that way about it. Besides, he told me he likes you."

Whenever Joan turned that level, intelligent, appealing gaze on her, Vicki had a hard time refusing.

"Joan, you could persuade a—a fish to carry an umbrella."

"Some fish need an umbrella. For instance, no self-respecting filet of sole would be caught without—I'm silly. Rest now, Vicki. I'll call you a few minutes before dinner."

"I won't look very grand, just in my flight uniform."

"Don't worry. Dad and I never dress up."

When Vicki came downstairs, a little before seven, the house was aglow with lighted lamps. Outside, the soughing of pines in the night wind, and the swish of waves, made the warm lighted house seem a real haven. A haven out of which the Purnells could be swept by the fortunes of a business, Vicki reflected.

Vicki hesitated at the door of the living room, for she heard the voices of Mrs. Purnell and Joan.

"—so selfish! Running away! How *could* you be so selfish?" Mrs. Purnell was saying. "You never once gave a thought to your father and me!"

"I'm sorry, Mother. I was selfish. I'm sorry for it."

"Besides, what possible reason could you have to run away? Don't we do everything to make you happy? You are a ridiculous child!"

"Mother!"

"When I was a girl, no one behaved so badly."

Vicki could hear Joan's sharp intake of breath. Then came Mr. Purnell's slow footsteps through another door, and his voice, saying quietly:

"Arabella, that will do."

Vicki felt horribly embarrassed to have overheard. But she had better seize this lull and enter the room or she might be an unwilling witness to still more. She rapped lightly on the doorframe and sang out:

"May I come in?"

"Certainly you may," Mr. Purnell said cheerfully.

"We are waiting for you." He came forward and took her arm, drawing her into the room. He smiled at Vicki, and patted Joan on the shoulder. In his comfortably shabby suit, with his thoughtful and kindly face, he was a comforting presence.

"I'm sorry I lost my temper at Joan, but I'm just so upset, Carter," Mrs. Purnell said, still almost unaware of Vicki. "But, Carter, you're never home any more, because of that business, and without you everything's so confused—I can't manage without you!" She looked like a child about to cry.

"There, there, darling." Joan's father turned to the two girls. "Not a very gay household this evening, are we? Well, dinner should cheer us up. In your honor, Vicki, and as a matter of local pride, we are having a Virginia ham. The left-hand ham, please note. Not the right leg—oh, no. The pig scratches himself with his right leg and this grows muscular. The left ham is the more tender, you see."

At the table Vicki peered at the rosy ham, encrusted with brown sugar, studded with cloves. She confessed:

"I can't tell whether it's left or right."

Mr. Purnell looked up from carving. "Difficult, very difficult."

Vicki began to grin, and she saw that Joan was silently laughing. Only Mrs. Purnell wrinkled her handsome brow.

"I don't understand, Carter. How could we ever find out whether a certain pig scratched itself or not? It seems unlikely."

"Most unlikely, Arabella, and will you serve the yams? Yams and hams, Joanie. There's a fine, juicy phrase for you."

"Yams aren't juicy," Mrs. Purnell protested.

"Oh, Mother. Dad's teasing!"

"Is he? Why, Carter. Why didn't you tell me?"

As dinner progressed, Vicki gathered something of the Purnells' life and circumstances. Apparently Mr. Purnell had a modest private income on which, with care, the family lived. Vicki suspected that he was neither strong nor practical. He had always spent his time in scholarly pursuits and from his conversation she recognized that he brought intensive learning to his work. He could easily have qualified as a professor, or even as curator of a museum. Birds were his especial study: he was completing the editing for the classical work of Audubon.

"That explains all the beautiful bird prints on the walls," Vicki said.

"It also explains Dad's garden," Joan said. "Come here in the spring and meet our feathered friends."

"And that's why he won't let me have a kitten," Mrs. Purnell put in. "He loves birds so. Anything that flies, you know."

They talked and laughed throughout dinner. But

the laughter was a little too prolonged, and grew strained. Vicki sensed again the tension in this house.

After coffee beside the fire in the sitting room, Mr. Purnell said he thought he would write letters in the library. He excused himself, looking troubled and withdrawn.

The three ladies remained sitting before the fire. Joan stared into the flames. Mrs. Purnell poured more coffee for them all, busy with her thoughts. Then she said suddenly to Joan:

"Has Dad heard from Jim Badger? Do you know?"

"He hasn't heard that I know of, Mother."

Mrs. Purnell turned to Vicki. "Jim Badger is my husband's partner, you know."

Joan and her mother, between them, told Vicki how the unlikely combination of Mr. Purnell and a lumber business had come about. Not long ago a relative had died and left Mr. Purnell a large timber tract in the interior of North Carolina, near a town called Slick Pond. Mr. Purnell had been advised that it was a valuable tract, containing hickory and second-growth ash, as well as less valuable trees.

"You know what ash is?" Joan said. "I read up on timber. Ash is used—bent—to make skis, golf clubs, oars, and a great many other things," Joan explained. "A lot of it is shipped to South America. The hickory is quite valuable, too."

"I flew over the Carolinas recently," Vicki remarked.

"Yes, I did see the forests. Got a lecture on them, as a matter of fact!"

"That's interesting," Mrs. Purnell said eagerly. "You've actually seen the timber tracts! Joan and I have never been down there. Mr. Purnell went down when he first inherited the business. I keep telling Dad he should go again."

"Dad would like to visit the mill again, Mother, but he's so busy with his end of the business, here. Besides, Dad was satisfied with his original visit. He said Jim Badger showed him absolutely everything, and the mill seemed well run. And Dad saw how Jim Badger is respected by all the other lumbermen."

"Yes, Dad came home quite enthusiastic."

Joan said thoughtfully, "I'm curious to see the mill and the forests myself. Jim Badger tells us, Vicki, that the tract was partly cut over, years ago, but most of it is practically a virgin forest. For that reason it's extremely valuable. That's what I don't understand—" bafflement filled Joan's face—"how this lumber business can be so valuable and still impoverish us."

Mrs. Purnell said idly, "Mr. Purnell inherited Jim along with the business, in a way."

"Not exactly," Joan said gently. "This is the way things happened."

But Mrs. Purnell gracefully stood up, saying she was tired and did not want to hear any more about the lumber business anyhow. The girls rose, too. She said good night to them, and went upstairs to her room.

Vicki and Joan were left alone together.

"Aren't you going to tell me the rest?" Vicki said. "You can't whet my interest and then stop! Unless it's confidential?"

Joan went on to tell Vicki the whole story, or as much of it as she knew. She was more self-possessed than she had been on the plane, and now the jumbled facts about Mr. Purnell's lumber business began to fall into place.

Jim Badger played an important part in the business. He worked down in Slick Pond, North Carolina, and also out of an office in Charleston, South Carolina. He did the actual running of the lumber mill, where the huge logs were cut into boards. Badger also ran the business end and did the shipping, sending the boards from the forest, via railroad, to the seaport. In this case the seaport was Norfolk, because the lumber was headed for Great Britain via a North Atlantic route.

In Norfolk, Mr. Purnell attended to receiving the lumber from the railroads and getting it transferred to ships, which carried it to Great Britain. The work was unfamiliar and difficult for the scholarly man and kept him extremely busy.

"First let me describe Jim Badger!" Joan interrupted herself. "You might think of Jim as being a boy, but I guess he's almost middle aged. He's a lot of fun, sort of hearty, like a sportsman. Always has his hair falling over his forehead, and he flushes like a kid if you tease him."

"You seem to like him," Vicki said.

"Oh, everybody likes Jim, you can't help liking Jim." Joan smiled. "Of course, he's really shrewder than he looks, and a good thing for Dad that he is."

They had all met when Jim came up to Norfolk to see Mr. Purnell at the time Mr. Purnell inherited the timber tracts. Jim Badger had been foreman and manager of the lumber mill for several years. He knew the business thoroughly. Mr. Purnell understood nothing of it. Jim Badger had said to him, "I can run it for you." Shortly thereafter, Jim had suggested that Mr. Purnell take him in as a partner, without investment. Joan's father was glad enough to do so, even relieved. A few weeks of trying to run the lumber business, even with the assistance of an experienced clerk, had been hard enough. But then the clerk had been taken ill, and left Mr. Purnell alone and bewildered.

"Miss Spry, the clerk's name is. Miss Matilda Spry." Joan shook her head. "There's a character for you! Dad inherited her along with the business. Miss Spry is an old maid, about a thousand years old, and she's been working in this lumber business all her life. She's technically a rate clerk, I guess, but there's nothing about the business she doesn't know. She really is wonderful! Sort of snappish, but nice underneath, and she certainly helped Dad! As long as Miss Spry was around, Dad's business went all right."

"And then Miss Spry got sick?"

"Yes, poor soul. When Dad inherited the business, he needed someone to help him. Jim Badger sent Miss Spry up here from Charleston, and the change of climate—it's colder here than in Charleston—may be what affected her health. Though it may have been, too, all those years of work telling on her."

"Poor woman."

"It's a shame." Joan went on regretfully, "At any rate, Miss Spry seemed to be headed for a breakdown. The doctors said she had to go west at once."

"That's a shame—for Miss Spry, and incidentally for your father, too."

Joan sighed. "She certainly has left a big hole in Dad's life. He had no knowledge of the lumber business and he was depending on her for everything, at least until he gained some experience. Miss Spry knew the answer to anything that came up. As a matter of fact, Dad has been so desperate since she left that he's tried communicating with her, only to have her doctor write that she was too ill to be troubled with business matters."

"I can see," Vicki said, "how her going must have really left your father in the lurch."

"Let's go in the library and cheer him up."

Joan led Vicki through the hall, and opened a door under the stairs. Joan poked her head in.

"May Vicki and I come in and visit you?"

"Certainly, certainly, my dears."

Vicki held back, feeling an intruder on family secrets. But Joan pressed her arm, and gave her a significant look. They went in.

The library was a tiny square room, and very much Mr. Purnell's. It had his desk and chair and lamp in the window, in front of the fireplace an ancient black horsehair chaise longue, four walls crowded with books, and nothing else.

Joan's father sat down in his desk chair, and Joan and Vicki sat side by side on the chaise, facing him.

"Now, Joanie, tell me truthfully. Why did you run away?"

"Because there's such a strained atmosphere here at home and Mother was irritable and you were so preoccupied and I—well, I lost my head. I suppose I ran away because I felt sorry for myself."

"Yes, I see. You're getting down to first causes."

Mr. Purnell smiled at Joan as he pushed aside the papers on his desk, with a tired gesture.

"Oh, for Miss Spry! I hope she gets back her health —before it's too late." He leaned back in his desk chair, tapping one foot. "I didn't want this business," he said ruefully.

"It was wished on me. I am not a businessman by

profession. All I seem to be getting out of this business is worries."

He turned troubled eyes on his daughter, and smiled a little at Vicki. Vicki kept silent, not knowing what to say, and sensing that it was a relief for Mr. Purnell to talk to them.

"It's rather a strange thing, how my situation has changed virtually overnight. Things were running smoothly, and then Miss Spry dumped everything in my lap, helter-skelter. Since she left, Jim Badger is sending greater and greater quantities of lumber up here to Norfolk, for me to put on boats. The lumber, everything, is piling up. I wonder if I shall ever catch up with it." Mr. Purnell rubbed his broad brow. "All this is happening so fast. So very fast. Sometimes I suspect things are happening faster than I realize."

Vicki was disturbed by the ominous note in his voice.

"Do you realize, Joan," her father went on unhappily, "that the lumber never came so fast before? Jim's freight shipments were spaced, and leisurely—when Miss Spry was with me. But now the lumber is just pouring in. I'm swamped with it." He gave another shove to the heap of papers on his desk.

Joan could contain herself no longer.

"Get rid of the tiresome, troublesome old business!" Joan cried. "Sell it and forget it! For goodness' sake, Dad, since we don't actually need it, let it go! It's only wearing you out and sharpening all our tempers!"

"And sending me to the poorhouse," Mr. Purnell observed. "That is, until I learn to run the business. But, Joan, you're being too impulsive. After all, you're growing up, a young lady needs many things. And this business is my big chance to get them for you.

"Besides, Joanie, I have the experienced Jim Badger to help me. Jim means a great deal to me. With him, I can't fail. On that one trip of mine to Slick Pond, he reassured me. No, Joan, I had better make the most of this big chance." He smiled at her, and at Vicki.

"But didn't you say," Vicki ventured, "that the business is losing money? *Costing* you money?"

He frowned. "I admit things are not going well, and that I don't understand why. But that undoubtedly is only temporary. Jim Badger is competent. I am learning my end of the job—soon I'll be able to—to—"

He sat with his chin cupped in his hand, face furrowed.

"What, Dad? What is it?"

"Nothing."

"But you look so distressed! Please tell me!"

But Joan's father remained immovable. When the girls rose and said good night, he barely nodded to them. They went upstairs, wondering.

At the top of the stairs, the two friends parted and Vicki went to her room. It was hazy with moonlight. She hesitated, then did not put on the light, but went to stand at the windows. She could hear the night sea rumbling. The inrushing waves, with their foaming white crests, pounded up on the beach, like white horses with wild manes flying.

She stood there a long time, sharply breathing in salt sea and pine. Mr. Purnell's story moved through her mind. It was coherent, yet it did not make sense. Where had the facts struck a snag? What was it Mr. Purnell was not telling? Or did not know, himself?

Vicki shivered. It was cold and late and she had work to do tomorrow. Lighting a lamp, she started to prepare for bed and then noticed she had not brought her handbag upstairs with her. It had her toothbrush in it.

"Bother! Let's see, now. I had it when Mrs. Purnell, Joan, and I were talking in the living room. I took it into the library and put it on Mr. Purnell's desk. Must still be there."

Vicki tiptoed down the stairs and found the ground floor dark and quiet. Under the stairs, she located the library door and let herself in. She groped to Mr. Purnell's desk and switched on the lamp.

On the floor lay her handbag and, near it, lay a crumpled piece of paper. Without thinking, she picked it up and glanced at the scribbling on it. There was much figuring, and underlined, the despairing phrase: "Need $25,000. Need $25,000."

Vicki went to bed but she could not sleep. What a sum! The Purnells certainly were in serious trouble!

"I wish so much that I could help them! But I'm no business person. How can I help? If I could get information on how lumber businesses are run— Yes, that might be the best way I could help."

And on that thought she closed her eyes and slept.

CHAPTER VIII

Moose and Mr. McQurg

ON THE TWO P.M. RUN BACK TO NEW YORK, NEXT DAY, Dean came back into the passenger cabin and sat down for a few minutes beside Vicki.

"Missed you last evening. Captain Jordan said you phoned him you were staying overnight at the Purnells'. What's happening with your friends?" Dean inquired.

Vicki, with one eye on her passengers, rapidly told him what she had learned.

"That business is ruining Mr. Purnell! And he can't figure out why!"

Dean gave a low whistle. "You know, that reminds me of a case Pete Carmody investigated for his newspaper. May not be a bit like your Purnells', but—"

Dean described a partnership in which one partner had forced the other out of the business. The dishonest one deliberately tried to ruin the business—incurred losses, piled up unnecessary expense, antagonized customers. The honest partner could not afford to take such a loss and so was forced to leave the business altogether. That left the dishonest partner in sole ownership. He then proceeded to "pick up the pieces" and rebuild the business for himself. The worst of such a maneuver, Dean pointed out, was that it was within the law, and difficult to prove dishonest.

"Vic, you say this Jim Badger has a shipping office in Charleston? Besides the one in Slick Pond? Maybe my father knows Badger, or could look him up."

Vicki tugged at a lock of fair hair. "Maybe. But looking up Jim Badger might embarrass Mr. Purnell." She explained that Mr. Purnell had gone down to Slick Pond, on inheriting the business, had investigated it and seen how Jim Badger worked. Mr. Purnell had full confidence in his partner. It occurred to Vicki that the rush of lumber shipments coincided with Miss Spry's leaving. But her mind turned to another possibility.

"Dean, remember flying me over the timber tracts?"

"Certainly I remember. In the Carolinas."

"Do you know the little town of Slick Pond?"

"Heard of it. About a hundred miles north of Charleston. Lumber mills all around there."

"Well, then," Vicki said excitedly, "what would you think of—well, flying down to Slick Pond to see what we could learn?"

Dean's serious face slowly lit up. "That's an inspired

idea! We'll do it on the first free time we have. Get a map of the tract."

After the plane landed in New York, the first thing Vicki did was to hurry to the Stewardesses' Lounge and write Joan Purnell a letter, asking Joan to send a map of their timber tract.

That done, Vicki looked for any incoming mail. She found a note from Ruth Benson: "Report to me immediately."

"Oh, dear, she's going to scold me for my sins," Vicki worried, trotting along. "Which sin, I wonder?"

But when Vicki pushed open the door of the assistant chief stewardess's office, her adored "Benny" beamed at Vicki out of those brilliant gray eyes.

"Come in. How's Vicki today? I have a special assignment for you—should really be fun. Wish I could take it myself."

Miss Benson handed her a typewritten directive. Vicki read it and blinked.

"What's this, Miss Benson? I'm going moose hunting?"

"Your passengers are going moose hunting. A group of businessmen are flying up to Canada in one of our charter planes, to hunt. You'll be their stewardess. The host—the one who's engaging the plane—is a Mr. Gordon McQurg."

That was how Vicki happened to be shaking hands with a large, grizzled, red-faced man, early Saturday morning, before a waiting plane. He wore rough clothes: checked hunting shirt and pants, Maine boots, an old felt hat, and he had a 30-caliber rifle slung on his shoulder. Gordon McQurg reminded Vicki of a huge, shaggy bear: friendly, but best not provoked.

As a host, McQurg roared at several men to "get out out of the car—get out of the car—get out here in the fresh air and sunshine! Where in thunder are old Donaldson and his carful? Come on out, you won't freeze!"

Four men emerged from McQurg's limousine into the chill of this early December morning. They were citified-looking men, sleek and pale, dressed like their host in hunting clothes. But Mr. McQurg's gun and boots obviously had seen use, while his guests' bright-hued garments were immaculately fresh from the store.

The guests had, besides, equipped themselves with shiny new Indian pack boots, shiny new high-top rubber boots, shiny new cavalry boots, ammunition in special cartridge boxes, horns to call the moose, compasses, waterproof matchboxes, field glasses, fancy hats and caps, ear flaps, thermometers, shiny new knives, shotguns, pistols, and rubber cushions. Vicki noticed one skinny man, staggering under his load of gadgets, who looked definitely unhappy about the whole thing. The guests acted extremely brisk and cheerful, and handled their guns with gingerly care.

Gordon McQurg strode among them, backslapping and booming. "Weather's perfect. Be in Canada in a

jiffy. Splendid crew, splendid plane. Sight ourselves a
fine critter before noon, what d'ye say? By Jupiter,
here's old Donny! About time!"

Another limousine drove up to the edge of the airfield. Half a dozen heavily laden men climbed out.
There were greetings, introductions, hearty sporting
talk, compliments to the host for devising this expedi-
tion. McQurg cut them short and herded his guests
aboard.

Vicki tried to seat the men, instructed them to strap
in, offered chewing gum—until she was genially
brushed aside by McQurg. "No time for all that!" he
ruled. She retired, a bit dashed, to her jump seat. The
plane got up and away quickly. Vicki at once went into
her sky kitchen to prepare breakfast trays.

She came out in a few minutes with a filled tray in
her hands, feeling for a footing on the plane floor.

"Miss—uh—little girl!"

"Yes, Mr. McQurg?"

He motioned her to bend down and said hoarsely in
her ear: "Don't know all my guests. Told my friends to
bring *their* friends. Introduced 'em to me at the airport, but darned if I can remember their names. Get
their names as you serve, and come back and point 'em
out to me."

He did not want her manifest. "Y-yes, sir."

Vicki hastily decided on a souvenir menu as the most
tactful method. She rigged up a tray as a writing board,

clipped a big sheet of airline paper on it, and wrote with a flourish across the top "Souvenir, McQurg Hunt Flight" and the date.

Then, as she brought out breakfast trays, Vicki asked each man to sign his name. In the process, Vicki could not help overhearing bursts of conversation:—"Chicago wheat pit, this week end, but that's speculative" —"will float a loan to Ecuador, provided our State Department"—"going to build three new cargo ships"— "how do you shoot this contraption, anyhow?" For moose hunters, Vicki considered, these men in fancy hunt costume talked as if they were still in their offices. The only cries of "Moose!" came from McQurg.

"Yes, sir," McQurg bellowed over the roar of the plane, "I've walked a good eighteen, twenty miles day after day, without even seeing the critters!"

"You have?" his guests said politely, weakly.

"Why, the guides have called 'em for hours but no results. Moose call goes like this—" and McQurg grunted and groaned. "But sometimes the moose isn't in the mood."

"What do you do then?" quavered the skinny man.

"Just walk a piece more."

"How far is that?"

"Oh—'nother eighteen, twenty miles," McQurg answered cheerfully.

His guests appeared to shrivel among their guns and thermometers and knapsacks.

By the time breakfast was over, and the plane well on its way north, Vicki had garnered two pieces of information which interested her very much. An older, gray-haired man, a Mr. Roland, was a Norfolk banker. Gordon McQurg himself was a lumber tycoon. Working in her galley, Vicki thought of Mr. Purnell—the needed loan—the needed information— Perhaps this flight was to be her opportunity to help Joan's father.

CRASH!

Vicki jumped. She heard shouts and felt a rush of icy air. As fast as she could, she hastened into the cabin. At the same time, young Johnson, today's copilot, ducked through the pilots' steel door, alarm in his face.

"What happened?"

"Blithering idiot let his gun go off! Through the window!" McQurg hollered. "Don't worry, I'll pay for it. Some hunter! Look out or the moose will shoot you!"

The wretched would-be hunter shivered from shame and fear beside the window, which had a neat, round hole in it. The men all laughed long and loud, but Vicki noticed they laid their guns in safer positions.

Young Johnson announced over the engine roar: "This is not funny, gentlemen! Unless you behave yourselves, we cannot take responsibility for continuing the flight!" And the young man fixed McQurg with a fearless eye.

McQurg sputtered. "Why, you impudent young—! Can't you see we're only relaxing?" The lumber tycoon was anything but relaxed, red in the face, ready to burst with annoyance at everyone around him.

"Sorry, sir, but the airline has its rules and they are for your safety." With that, Johnson marched out.

Vicki, straight-faced, covered the hole in the window with strips of adhesive tape and tried to restore peace and tempers by passing around a box of cigars and newspapers. But McQurg, incensed, could not sit still. He paced, or rather staggered, up and down the aisle. Booming at his guests, trying to be the playful host, he exasperatedly could not remember the names Vicki had repeated to him. He kept consulting his watch.

"Great day, aren't we ever going to get there? How long is this run? What is this, a perambulator? Having fun, everybody?"

Vicki wanted to talk lumber with him, and finally she got an opportunity. But at this moment, Copilot Johnson came back to report to McQurg.

"We've developed a slight mechanical difficulty, sir. We'll have to make a landing."

"Come down? Nothing of the sort! Keep 'er flying! Who's giving orders here?"

"The pilot is, sir. Sorry, Mr. McQurg, but the repair should take only twenty minutes or so."

They came down on a landing strip in the middle of nowhere. The strip had been constructed by one of the Canadian lines for just such emergency landings.

The repairs took two hours. In that two hours the erstwhile hunters lost what festivity they had had. They huddled forlornly around a bonfire in this bare, wind-swept field and frankly talked business. No one even mentioned moose.

Gordon McQurg was past being able to talk. He strode up and down, all by himself, gun clanking, muttering under his breath. He puffed furiously on one cigar after another. Every two minutes he consulted his watch and bellowed: "Delay! Delay! Just when the weather is perfect for hunting! And nobody gives a hoot except me. Why—why—why, they don't deserve a moose!"

The only response the other men made was to move back into the plane, where it was warmer. Vicki heated coffee, and served the remains of the breakfast supplies, calling it lunch. Someone started a card game, and invited McQurg to join in. But McQurg, out for a holiday, could not relax.

"Mr. McQurg." It was Vicki, timidly.

"Well? Well? What is it?"

She smiled up at him, with all the kind-sir-please-help-me air she could muster.

"I wonder if I might ask your advice?"

The big man looked down at her, like a bear just discovering a very small, pleading squirrel.

"If you don't mind my asking, Mr. McQurg?"

His bad temper subsided and he said quite kindly, "No, no, always glad to give advice—if I can, and if it's wanted. What's your name again, little girl?"

Vicki suppressed a smile. "I'm Vicki Barr, and I—I'm a regular stewardess on Federal Airlines."

"Oho, so now she's standing on her dignity!" Gordon McQurg looked amused. He threw away his chewed-up cigar and gave Vicki his full attention. "Well, now, Miss Barr, what's this advice you want?"

"I understand you own a large lumber business, Mr. McQurg, and I—"

"I own the largest lumber business in the country!"

Vicki was appropriately impressed. "Then I'm very lucky to have met you. You see, I've been flying over timber tracts recently, and hearing talk about lumber businesses." Vicki discreetly mentioned no names. "I've been trying to understand it."

Gordon McQurg was glad to talk lumber, and flattered to play teacher. He ordered Vicki to sit down with him on the ground. Then he gave her a complete, succinct, authoritative analysis of the branches of the industry, and how each branch functions. Vicki had to admire his thorough knowledge.

"Suppose, Mr. McQurg, that a lumber business had a good tract and plenty of orders, and still was failing. What would you say was wrong?"

"Poor management. Especially in the shipping. If

the railroad or ocean shipments were handled badly, that would eat up the profits."

Vicki remembered that Mr. Purnell handled the ocean shipping: he was new at it, and might be inefficient. Or Jim Badger, who did the railroad shipping, might be at fault.

She asked other questions. Gordon McQurg talked to her intensively for an hour, giving her a gold mine of information—about shipping, freight rates, demurrage, storage rates, types of timbers, but stressing the shipping. This information could be a great help to Mr. Purnell. Vicki stored it all away in her memory. She was really very grateful to McQurg. And the man was enjoying himself. In fact, when the pilot announced, "Flight will now be resumed!" the hunter groaned at the prospect of returning to his tenderfoot guests.

"If I'd known 'em, I wouldn't've invited 'em," he confided to Vicki. "Now I suppose the weather will be awful and there'll be no game. And I'm stuck with 'em for a week. Bah! I'm already sick of 'em."

He strode back into the plane.

When the plane landed at McQurg's private airfield in the wilds of Canada, early that afternoon, the lumber tycoon clumped off in disgust. The others straggled after him, picking their way fastidiously in their shiny new boots through mud and snow toward a hunting lodge. Their costumes looked very new and gaudy here in the northern woods. McQurg was too disgusted even to turn around to see if they were coming. Vicki watched, giggling. She could imagine what the moose would think.

"If they're hunters," said Johnson, "I am king of the Eskimos."

Vicki and the two pilots flew the plane back to Chicago, where it was needed to go out on a commercial flight. Without cargo or passengers, aided by favorable winds, they made rapid time. They arrived in Chicago that same afternoon. Vicki spent another hour in the hangar, checking over her plane and writing out her reports.

She had visions of a hot dinner and a comfortable hotel room, with a flight right out, tomorrow morning. But she found a telegram waiting for her in the Stewardesses' Lounge.

"Report Flight No. 7 Chicago to New York Sunday evening 6 P.M. Ruth Benson."

She had practically all day Sunday off. Why, she could go home to Fairview! Vicki forgot she was hungry and tired. She ran to catch a local train.

CHAPTER IX

Quick Visit Home

THE LOCAL TRAIN DOWN TO FAIRVIEW CONSISTED OF A small engine with a shrill whistle, a milk car, and two rattling coaches. Banging along for two hours on this Toonerville Trolley, Vicki never felt sure when or if she would get to her destination. But the engine's biting soft-coal smoke, and Mr. Stark, the ancient conductor who knew every passenger, made Vicki feel she was already home.

Arriving at 6:00 P.M., more or less on time, Vicki stepped off the train at the Fairview platform, and right into the midst of her old high school crowd. Here were Dickie Brown, still clowning but grown taller and handsomer—his amiable sister, Lynn, whom Vicki had sat next to at school, because both their names began with B—Tootsie Miller, and she was still jolly and still too fat—the Kramer boys with their guitars—Guy English, leading a setter pup on a brand-new leash—

Vicki greeted them delightedly, as they all swarmed around her.

"Vicki Barr! Look at the flight uniform! You actually *do* come back to the sticks!"

"Of course I come back to Fairview—and always will!"

"Vicki, how you've grown up!"

Dickie sang out, "Mr. Stark, hold the train for us, please?"

"Where are you going?" Vicki asked, a bit wistfully. She was so glad to see their familiar faces. It made her homesick, made her want to go along with them.

"Where're we going? Why, it's Saturday night—have you forgotten, Vic? We're going down to Tootsie's uncle's farm for supper and a barn dance."

"The Blue Shirt Dance?" Vicki breathed.

The boys opened their overcoats to display blue shirts. "None other. Come with us. Come on, Vic! Bet you New York hasn't any barn dances."

Mr. Stark called out testily, "Get on, young'uns! The milk's a-spoilin'."

Vicki was torn between desiring to go home and yearning to go along to the Blue Shirt Dance. "Next time," she said reluctantly. "Have fun!"

Her old crowd clambered aboard. "Meet us in the candy store tomorrow morning, Vicki, and we'll tell you what you missed!"

The train clattered off, and Vicki caught a bus out to the edge of town, and The Castle.

Out of the quiet and shadows, her house loomed up on the hill. She looked hungrily at its tower rising among bare tree branches and early stars. Vicki quickened her steps, and finally was running up the road, and up the curving driveway. All the lights were on downstairs—good, that meant her family was home! She rang *tum-tum-te-tum-tum* at the barred oaken door—the family signal—and the door opened in a flash.

"Vicki! Vicki herself!" Ginny cried.

"Ginny herself!" Vicki pulled her little sister's braids and caught her up in a hug. Mrs. Barr came hurrying out into the entrance hall, laughing and tossing back her short curls.

"Honey, this is marvelous! What a nice surprise. No luggage? Just a short stay?"

"Just till tomorrow afternoon, dear." Vicki kissed her mother. "What do you know?—I'm glad to see you!"

Her mother kissed her in return. "Oddly enough, I'm glad to see you, too."

Freckles, their white brown-spotted spaniel, bounded and barked at Vicki's feet. She bent down to stroke him. A door at the top of the stairs opened. Professor Barr stepped out of his study holding a sheaf of quiz papers. His red pencil looked ominous, but Vicki's father, who was tall and blond, looked extremely pleasant.

"Victoria?"

"Hello, Dad! Give all your students A's and come on down."

"Well, I'll come down. This is fine, fine, Victoria!"

"Had your supper, dear?"

"I'll cook, Betty!" the professor eagerly told his wife.

"Oh, no, you don't. You are a Sunday cook only."

Ginny peered at Vicki severely from behind her glasses. Ginny, who was twelve and plump, and who was temporarily enduring glasses, braces on her teeth, and orthopedic oxfords (all of which Vicki had gone through not so long ago), could look quite severe.

"Didn't you bring Freckles a present? Look how disappointed he is!"

The little spaniel was sniffing and whimpering around Vicki's overnight bag, pawing it to get it open. Baffled, he sat up with his forepaws lifted, and looked imploringly at Vicki.

"You have a heart of stone," Ginny accused.

Vicki said weakly, "Freckles can have my comb and brush to play with." She got them out for him, and the spaniel joyously batted them under the living-room couch. "But I haven't any free samples for you this time, Ginny."

"That's all right. I collected free samples of marshmallows, shoe polish, and baby talcum this week. Hey, I think the parents want us."

They went into the dining room, and after Vicki had

been fed, all four Barrs moved into the long living room. Lewis Barr lit a fire, and they sat exchanging news. Vicki reported on her work, and the longed-for assignment to Mexico, and told them about her friends, the Purnells. Ginny admitted she was not doing so well in economics class, which was a family disgrace, since their father was professor of economics at the near-by State University. He, in turn, admitted he had been bested in the Gourmet and Skillet Club by another amateur chef, when his chocolate soufflé unfortunately exploded. Betty Barr had been riding a half-broke mare from Killian's stables. Freckles's only recent exploit of note had been to tangle with the Walkers' cat, but now he and the cat were friends.

After discussion of Fairview doings, the world situation (courtesy of the professor), and a decision that Vicki had better take the two-thirty train tomorrow afternoon, it was way past time to go to bed. One of the things Vicki had always appreciated in her family was that they loved to stay up late as much as she did.

Vicki awoke next morning to find Freckles sitting on her chest and Ginny perched on the foot of her bed.

"The lake's frozen over!" Ginny announced. "Let's go skating."

"All right." Vicki yawned. "If you're sure it's frozen solid. But first let's go downtown and see who's in the candy store. I'll ask Dad for the car."

"Car's at the garage for repairs."

They took the bus, stopped to buy extra newspapers, and breakfasted in the candy shop on fried-egg sandwiches. Vicki's old crowd was congregated there. They reported the Blue Shirt Dance had been pretty good, but not like the old dances, since so many of their friends had scattered.

"It's better in the summer," Tootsie Miller said, "People come back for vacations, then."

"Maybe next summer," Vicki said, "we can all have a real reunion. For Fourth of July—a real bang-up party."

Ginny tugged at Vicki's sleeve. "Ice skating," she hissed. "You haven't much time."

But back at The Castle, Vicki begged off for a few minutes. She wanted to wander through the sweeping front lawn and the frosty garden, where roses and peonies and rock-garden flowers bloomed in warmer months—to look at the birdhouses the swallows had now deserted—to see the little woods behind their house which led downhill to the boathouse and lake. Vicki stole a few more minutes to wander through the house itself, which with its tower and casement windows and sunken living room was a storybook house. She loved this place.

"Lunch!" called their mother.

Ginny dropped her ice skates in the hall with a thump. "Another delay," she protested.

Vicki consoled her by telling them all at lunch of the ice show she had seen in New York. Ginny was fascinated. "I want to try the butterfly dance."

"A rather plump butterfly," her father teased.

On skates, Ginny was a rather plump but also a deft butterfly. Vicki at first would not put on her skates, insisting on inspecting the ice first. But Ginny pointed out that it was one o'clock, only an hour and a half before traintime, only an hour before Vicki must start preparing to leave.

"Guess the ice is solid enough," Vicki agreed, and sat down on a log and fastened on her skates. "Freckles, will you stop chewing on these straps? Call him, Ginny."

Ginny whistled and the three of them skidded out on the ice together. Vicki had not skated in a long time, and the long, easy strokes felt good. Ginny's strokes were even smoother than Vicki's. Only the spaniel was having trouble, sliding and falling and then wagging his tail to pretend nothing had happened.

"Let's skate together," Vicki called.

Her sister skated over, they joined hands crosswise, and were off. Vicki hummed a waltz for them to skate to. Presently Ginny broke free and did some creditable "eagle splits." Vicki tried a few gliding dance steps. They "snapped the whip" together.

"How did the butterfly steps go, Vic?"

"Something like this—only they had big wings—"

And Vicki executed some graceful, long, slow whirls.

"Like this?" Ginny repeated. She started turning and turning out on the ice, out toward the center of the lake.

"Not so fast!" Vicki called. "It was gentler—"

Ginny was whirling. She whirled faster and faster. Apparently she could not stop. Suddenly Vicki heard a cra-a-ack, a splash, and Ginny dropped out of sight.

"Ginny!"

Vicki skated over as fast as she could, then stopped short of the broken ice and water where Ginny's head bobbed. Ginny looked surprised and scared but she shouted:

"Stay away! Or you'll fall in, too!"

"Keep kicking your feet! Kick those heavy skates off, if you can!"

"And lose 'em?"

"Better than drowning." Vicki tore off her own skates, found a solid stretch of ice, and threw herself flat, as close to Ginny as the ice would allow. "Can you grab my hand? Freckles, go away!"

The excited spaniel barked around them and seized Vicki's outstretched hand in his teeth. He seemed to think all this a game, for his special benefit. Vicki pushed the little dog away and reached out again for Ginny. Freckles bounded up to lick her face.

"Freckles, you fool! Go away! Kick, Ginny."

"I—am—kicking."

"Reach for my hand."

Ginny reached, could not make it. Vicki wriggled over on her stomach, and again stretched out her hand. Ginny grabbed it, pulled, and Vicki pulled. In went Vicki into the water, head and shoulders. She quickly drew herself up and out, and yanked Ginny back, too. Ginny managed to catch hold of solid ice and scramble up.

Meanwhile, Freckles had fallen in. They fished him out. Then all three of them stood there dripping and looking foolishly at one another.

"We're—look at Freckles—I'm sorry, Vic—*kerchoo!*"

"You're soaked—get back to the house at once!" Vicki hurried Ginny back and carried Freckles in her arms.

Mrs. Barr was shocked, if not surprised, at her two wet, wretched daughters. It took them a long time to pull off wet clothes, dry out their hair, get dressed, and get warmed through again. Mr. Barr administered hot lemonades, and gave Freckles warm milk.

"Oh! My train! My *plane!* My six-o'clock plane!"

"You've missed the two-thirty train," her father said. "But there's a three-thirty train. That should get you into Chicago at five-thirty."

"Five-thirty—and then I have to drive to the airport—" Vicki figured desperately. "I'm supposed to be there an hour before flight time, to check over the plane. Well, that's out. I'll be lucky if I can make the plane at all!"

As she raced to get into flight uniform, Vicki wondered if she ought to notify the airline. Notify them of what? That she *might* not be on the six-o'clock plane? Pride held her back. And there was every chance she would be on it. The airline's instructions left a matter like this to individual judgment—and Vicki judged she had a good chance of getting there on time. Besides, it would take more precious minutes to send the message, or to instruct her family to send it. Vicki said the fastest good-bye on record to her family, and fled to catch the three-thirty train.

That local train tootled into Chicago ten minutes late. Vicki fell out of a taxi at the airport three minutes late. Just in time to see her plane's tiny lights winking away over Lake Michigan.

It was a miserable Vicki who next day reported to the New York office. She was ushered in, not to Ruth Benson, who was temporarily away, but to the superintendent himself. He was a stern man, not easy to deal with.

"Miss Barr, this is inexcusable! You should have notified us. You have put several people to great inconvenience."

Vicki hung her head. She could not say that she had been fishing a small sister and a spaniel out of an ice hole.

"Seriously, Miss Barr, you could be dismissed for this. Let me remind you that you are the youngest stewardess on this airline—that the admission rules were broken as an exception in your case—and that you must justify that exception by good performance!"

Vicki felt terribly unhappy. She knew that what the superintendent said was fully justified. The reprimand went on, and for the first time in her life Vicki thought it might be convenient to die. Here and now, if possible.

"Miss Barr, we are going to suspend you for a week, without salary. And please realize that this goes into your permanent record."

Vicki crept out of his office, in disgrace.

CHAPTER X

Part of the Answer

ON THE DAY SHE WAS SUSPENDED, TWO LETTERS AWAITED Vicki in the airline's office. One, addressed to the airline by Mr. Purnell, had been routed to Vicki. In the highest terms, he praised the young stewardess's perception, tactful handling, and sense of responsibility in the rescue of his runaway daughter. It helped a little to lift Vicki out of her official state of disgrace.

The other was a personal letter to Vicki from Joan. Vicki looked at it fondly—the dignified white paper marked "Purnell, Linkhorn Bay"—the large, impulsive, schoolgirlish handwriting.

"Dear Vicki"—Joan wrote—

"Forgive me for coming to you again with my troubles. There is no one else I can turn to.

"Dad's business suddenly got him into the most awful jam. It's a nightmare, Vicki. I don't know what we

112

*are going to do. Poor Dad is frantic. You can imagine
the effect on Mother.*

"*I need your help, Vicki. Come soon.*

Gratefully, Joan"

Vicki was alarmed. She thought wryly that being
suspended had its fortunate side: she was free to visit
the Purnells. She at once sent a telegram to Joan:
"Coming to see you five this afternoon. Keep a stiff up-
per lip. Vicki." She went out as a private passenger on
the Norfolk plane—her own run.

Vicki never remembered much of that particular
flight. Her thoughts raced ahead to the brown-fir house
between ocean and pine woods.

By five, out on the beach road, it was desolate, dark
and cold, with a near-gale blowing off the choppy
ocean. Vicki stood before the white door and dropped
the brass eagle knocker.

Mr. Purnell himself opened the door. He drew Vicki
in out of the wind, saying:

"Here she is! Come in, Victoria, you must be cold."

The house was warm and alight with lamps. But instantly Vicki felt the tension. It was in Mr. Purnell's
haggard face, and in Joan's strained voice as she came
running.

"Vicki! Oh, I'm so glad! You're going to stay overnight, of course. I insist, we all do."

The girl took Vicki's wraps and led her into the liv-

ing room. She explained that her mother had a head-
ache and was lying down. The three of them sat down
around the open fire.

"Victoria needs a cup of hot tea, Joanie," her father
reminded her.

"Oh! Of course." Joan rose quickly and arranged a
little tray for Vicki, from tea things on the large table,
and brought it over.

"You're the nicest waitress I ever saw," Vicki said,
trying to evoke a smile.

But Joan did not look well. There was an old expression on her young face, and her velvety brown eyes
had a fixed, strained look.

"Well, Vicki," Mr. Purnell said with an effort, "tell
us what adventures you've been having."

Vicki did not mention her suspension—they were
having troubles enough of their own without hearing
hers. She described Ginny's falling through the ice,
making it as amusing as she could. Then, trying not to
sound presumptuous, she told Mr. Purnell about Gordon McQurg and the information the lumberman had
given her. Vicki had memorized it well and she told it
well. She knew it could help Mr. Purnell. But whether
he was really listening, she could not know. He said
politely:

"That's most helpful, Vicki, thank you."

Mrs. Purnell's arrival cut short Vicki's quotation of
the lumberman on shipping routes. They all stood up

as Joan's mother entered. Anyone else's mother, Vicki thought, with a splitting head and crucial financial worries, would probably not be drifting idly around the house in a pink marabou negligee and smelling salts. Arabella Purnell was a picture of musical-comedy grief. But Mrs. Purnell had her entertainment value, at least judging by her husband's amused, fond smile.

"Vicki, my dear." Mrs. Purnell kissed her. "So nice to see you. Your room is all ready for you, too. Will someone close that open window, wherever it is?"

Joan attentively closed a window at the far end of the room.

"It's still chilly," Mrs. Purnell complained. "And, Joan, why are you wearing that awful dress?"

"Please, Mother—"

"Really, Joan, I think you wear it just to irritate me. Now look at the attractive frock Vicki has on."

Vicki squirmed along with Joan. Mrs. Purnell was peevish, and determined to find fault, today. Vicki's attempts to amuse her and get her mind off her troubles did not sweeten Arabella Purnell's mood or tongue.

Dinner, when the hour finally came, could only be described as an ordeal. Mr. Purnell's tall stories were missing tonight, Joan kept lapsing into troubled silence, even Mrs. Purnell's chatter ran thin. Vicki talked valiantly, trying to drive out the cold wind of worry. The table, though laden and gleaming with silver, crystal, food, gave no more impression of plenty than a death's-head. Vicki would not have been surprised if some evil genie whisked it all away, leaving a bare table and a crust of bread. Perhaps Mrs. Purnell, as she stared at the silver, was thinking of it on the auctioneer's table.

After dinner, Mr. Purnell limped away to the library, and Mrs. Purnell wandered aimlessly around, snapping at Joan. Joan decided it wisest to keep out of her mother's way. She whispered to Vicki, "Let's go up to your room and talk."

They asked Joan's mother if she would excuse them, and went upstairs to the charming room. For a few minutes they looked out at the inlet, but Joan wanted to talk. She came right to the point.

"Dad owes twenty-five thousand dollars, and unless he raises it within a few days we'll lose this house— and everything we own!"

The crux of the matter, Joan explained excitedly, was this: in the lumber business, a man could be wiped out financially if the lumber was shipped too fast and by anything but the shortest route.

Purnell's lumber mill seemed, from all indications, to be doing an enormous business. His partner, Jim Badger, was steadily shipping huge orders out of Slick Pond to Norfolk, to go to buyers in England. But in order to get the lumber off the railroad at Norfolk (so that it could be loaded onto ships bound for Great

Britain), Mr. Purnell was required to pay the railroads spot cash. The lumber was arriving in Norfolk so fast that Mr. Purnell did not have the money for the freight bill. Recently Jim Badger had sent a huge order of dimension lumber for Liverpool, and had run up a twenty-five thousand dollar freight bill.

"Dad hasn't twenty-five thousand dollars or any-thing remotely like it!" Joan burst out.

"But Jim Badger ran up that bill," Vicki said.

"Yes, but Jim's not liable for it. Dad is." Joan ex-plained: "When they formed their partnership, they made a special and rather unusual agreement. They agreed that the financing of the freight charges were to be Dad's responsibility, to offset Jim's years of ex-perience at lumbering." Joan's hands shook. "Dad alone is indebted for that sum!"

"Great heavens," Vicki said under her breath. "Couldn't your father raise that sum somewhere? Float a loan—at a bank—a business loan?"

"I'll tell you about that difficulty next! But first I want to show you something, Vicki."

Joan ran into her own room and returned with some railroad timetables of southern lines. On the backs of these timetables were maps showing the areas the railroad served. Tracing the lines with her finger, Joan indicated to Vicki the several routes available between Slick Pond and Norfolk, and the route that Jim Badger had chosen.

Vicki recalled what Gordon McQurg had told her, and saw Jim's error. He could have shipped the lumber fairly directly and quickly from Slick Pond, in the interior of North Carolina, to the coast and then straight up the Atlantic coast line to Norfolk. Instead, Jim Badger first sent the lumber due north, then transferred it northeast, then shuttled it due east to the coast, and finally to Norfolk. Badger's route was about half again as long as necessary.

"Why, this route must be fantastically expensive!" Vicki said. She wondered about the freight agent in this case. Mr. McQurg had said that freight agents helped shippers work out the best routes, advised, recommended, vetoed routes.

"Joan, has your father consulted a railroad agent about this questionable routing?"

"Yes, Dad has talked with the railroad agent up here in Norfolk. The agent says the routing does seem awfully roundabout and expensive, but that it isn't up to him. The railroad agent down in Slick Pond and Charleston—the one in the Carolina area—is the one who would approve Jim's routing, or suggest a better one."

"The Carolina agent would be the one Jim Badger deals with?"

"That's right," Joan said. "His name is Ganner. In fact, he's a friend of Jim's, Jim told Dad when he came up to see us. Jim and that railroad agent have been working together for years. I suppose that Ganner approves Jim's routing for some sound reason."

They fell to brooding. Then Vicki said slowly:

"But *why* is Jim shipping it in this costly manner?"

Joan shrugged. "It certainly is ruining Dad. Practically every day Dad has to pay hundreds of dollars for freight and—what d'you call it?—demurrage. And that means he has to borrow the money on short-term loans. Five-day, three-day, ten-day loans. Imagine it, Vicki!"

"Isn't there any way around those loans?"

"Dad explained to me that as soon as he gets the lumber aboard a ship, and gets his ocean bill of lading, he *ought* to be able to get a big, long-term loan that would cover him till the money comes in from the sale of the lumber. Then all his problems would be solved."

"Ought? He really could get a loan?"

"Certainly Dad could get a loan. It's routine. Dad explained to me that any business firm shipping lumber abroad gets trade acceptances, and the bank discounts these. A trade acceptance is a cash advance against the merchandise actually put on board the ship. That is, Dad should be able to get—in cash, mind you, immediately—eighty per cent in exchange for his tally and bills of lading."

Vicki did some quick figuring. Mr. Purnell was steadily shipping many thousands of dollars' worth of lumber on order to Great Britain. Eighty per cent of that amount surely would yield him the twenty-five thousand dollars he so urgently needed.

"Then why doesn't your dad get a loan?" Vicki inquired practically.

Joan started to laugh, but not humorously. When she calmed down, she explained that there was only one bank in Norfolk that Mr. Purnell had dealt with long enough to warrant his asking for a twenty-five-thousand-dollar loan. The head of the bank, a Mr. Roland, was out of town and in his absence Mr. Purnell had to wait.

"A Mr. Roland!" Vicki exclaimed. "Why, I—"

"Dad *can't* wait! Oh, it's infuriating, Vicki!" Joan rushed on. "Dad got a letter from the chief cashier at the bank, refusing Dad's request for an over-all, long-term loan, and making some lame excuse about the behavior of the British pound. The British pound, indeed! The cashier is just scared to act in Mr. Roland's absence."

Vicki told Joan how she personally had watched Mr. Roland disappear in the Canadian wilderness. It was irony that she herself had flown Mr. Roland out of Mr. Purnell's reach.

"Of all times for Mr. Roland to go moose hunting!" Joan mourned. "Of course we can't reach him. If we could, Dad could probably get his loan. But there's Mr. Roland up in Canada, miles from a telephone. And every day that goes by, Dad's situation grows worse."

Vicki thought with grim humor of the state Mr. Roland, Mr. McQurg's temper, and the moose must be in by now. She started to tell Joan, hoping to divert her, but Joan rushed on:

"If only that clerk, Miss Spry, would recover her health and come back! That would help Dad to some degree."

Vicki tugged at a lock of hair. "Well, then, can't you get Jim Badger to slow down the shipments?"

Joan shook her head. "Vicki, this is a kind of nightmare. Dad has tried and tried to reach Jim, and tell him to slow down those shipments. But he can't. I've been wiring Jim at his Charleston office, for Dad, to choose more economical routes. No answer from him. I've tried telephoning his Charleston office long-distance, but each time I'm told Jim Badger is out logging in Slick Pond. And there's no phone back there in the wilderness." Joan got up and paced the room.

Vicki watched her friend with concern. She did not like Joan's strained look. Joan had looked like that when Vicki caught her running away.

"Vicki, I'm going down to Charleston and Slick Pond myself!" Joan said wildly. "This can't wait! I've got to do something."

"Joanie, you're overexcited," Vicki said gently. "There wouldn't really be much use in your going down to Slick Pond. If anyone goes, it should be your father."

"He's too busy here in Norfolk to get down there. Day after day he makes the rounds of Chesapeake Bay and all its ports, to see what ships have arrived and what space they have—and if no ships are available, Dad has to store the lumber and that's another additional cost. Poor Dad! He's on the phone with freight agents all day long— Why, he can't go to Slick Pond!"

Then Joan confided that there was still another matter worrying the Purnells.

Jim Badger kept shipping cheap yellow pine to Norfolk, but never any of the much more valuable hickory or second-growth ash. Mr. Purnell could not understand it. He was positive there were hickory and ash on the Purnell tract, one of the few such tracts left in that area.

"Has your father ever consulted an attorney with the idea of checking on the deed to the tract?" asked Vicki.

"I believe Badger's lawyer did give Dad a report at one time," Joan replied. She bit her lip, thinking.

"Why aren't the hickory and ash ever shipped?" Joan asked curiously. "What's happening to Dad's really valuable timber?"

A heavy silence descended on the gay little room. Joan's face was clouded. Vicki felt distressed for her, and for all the Purnells. She thought hard, but the stubborn facts still did not add up to sense. There was a mysterious gap in this whole story.

"There's only one thing to do," Vicki said at last. "Your father—not you, Joan—should go down there and find out what's behind all this."

Joan nodded but repeated wretchedly that Mr. Purnell could not go. He had to remain here and raise the sum for which Jim had indebted him to the railroad or be ruined. Lose business, private income, home.

"Besides, Dad is actually a sort of hostage," Joan said. "He's unable to leave Norfolk because of the huge sums he's borrowed on those short-term loans, borrowed on his signature alone. Someone else will have to go to Slick Pond for him—and it should be me!"

Joan was so overwrought that Vicki decided it was high time to take a firm stand, and check the girl if possible. Vicki said aloud the thoughts and plans that had been crystallizing in her mind for some time:

"A while back I flew over the Carolina forests, with Dean Fletcher in his Piper Cub. You remember him, don't you, Joan? Well, Dean promised to fly me down to Slick Pond. I thought we could learn something at first hand. Now I've got time off, and Dean should be able to get some free time. I have the map of your father's tract which you mailed me." Vicki looked at Joan persuasively. "So you see, Joanie, you could give up your rather fruitless idea of going down there yourself."

"It isn't foolish!" Joan muttered, half to herself. But

she was quiet enough again for Vicki to feel reassured.

Vicki fell to thinking. She could not understand Badger's behavior. Didn't Jim Badger realize that his too-rapid shipments were ruining his partner? Or didn't he care?

"What was that story Pete told Dean, and Dean told me?" Vicki wrinkled her forehead. "Two partners, and —let's see—one ran down the business in order to drive out the other. Could Jim Badger be up to something like that?"

It was hard to tell. Suspicions were not enough to go on. She needed to get down to Slick Pond and Charleston, and find out how Jim Badger ran his end of the business. That might not be so simple. Honest or dishonest, Jim might resent her snooping.

Vicki glanced up to find Joan crying.

Vicki was appalled. She went over and put her arm around Joan. "There, Joanie. Don't take things so hard."

The girl looked up. Her eyes were swollen.

"Oh, Vicki, I'm so frightened."

"Don't cry, please don't cry."

Joan said huskily, "This business mess is going to break Dad, and be the finish of my family—unless something is done, and fast!"

"Joan, don't do anything rash. Don't do anything you'll regret!"

The girl had grown deathly pale.

"Joan," Vicki said urgently. "Listen to me! I'll get down to Slick Pond very soon. I promise you. Until then, wait."

"I can't wait, Vicki!"

"Please, Joanie, be reasonable."

But Joan Purnell shook her head.

CHAPTER XI

Rescue

THE FIRST THING VICKI DID WHEN SHE RETURNED TO NEW York next morning was to telephone Dean Fletcher.

"I'm arranging right now to get time off," Dean reassured her. "Yes, Vicki, I'll fly you down to Slick Pond soon. . . . How soon? Not sure, but maybe in a day or two . . . What? . . . Okay, Vic, I'll do my best.

"Oh—er—Vicki," he continued awkwardly, "don't let this suspension business get you down. I know how you feel. I've been in the doghouse myself more than once. But it's tough the first time you come up against the brass. I'll be seeing you."

Vicki's eyes were misty when she came away from the telephone. Good old Dean. She knew what an effort this pat on the back had been for the taciturn pilot. He would never know how much his awkward effort to show his understanding and sympathy meant to her.

Vicki had the apartment to herself all that Tuesday. The other stewardesses were out on flights. That fact, and Mrs. Duff's sharp glance, made Vicki feel the disgrace of her suspension all the more keenly. She slept most of the morning; by the afternoon she had lots of energy and nothing to use it for. She fled to the movies but the picture was about flying, and made her gloomier than ever. She wandered around the New York shops but, with no salary this week, that was not very cheering either.

Wednesday was happier. Vicki awoke to find that Charmion and Jean had come in from their runs during the night, and were asleep in the adjoining beds on either side of her.

At breakfast, the big topic was Vicki's week of suspension. Vicki did not wish to talk about her misery. But all the girls had heard what happened and were feeling badly about it, especially Charmion and Jean.

"It's awful to do this to you!" Jean asserted, running a hand through her crisp brown hair. "You're one of the best—here, have some bacon, sweetie—one of the very best stewardesses, and everybody knows it, and what if you did make an error? No one's perfect."

Charmion, pouring coffee, did not look as calm as usual. "Jean's right. It *is* awful. The superintendent is being much too hard on you. After all, Vicki, saving one's sister from drowning is a pretty adequate excuse."

Vicki had not said a word up till now. She squirmed, although she was touched at her friends' loyalty.

"Fishing Ginny out of the lake is my private life— and the airline isn't interested in that," she said dryly. "Business is business. I should have made my plane, no matter what."

"But the airline—any employer—does recognize—"

"I'll bet you didn't even tell the superintendent about dragging Ginny out of that icy lake! Did you?"

"Certainly not." Vicki held her head high. "I'm darned if I'm going to throw myself on anyone's mercy."

"Oh, Vicki, Vicki," Charmion chided. "You're much too proud."

"You're a goose," Jean said bluntly. "Here you have a perfectly good reason and you don't even mention it. The superintendent is tough, sure, but he'll listen to reason."

"He wouldn't have suspended you if he'd known," Charmion urged.

Vicki looked from one to the other, nearly ready to cry at their kindness and concern. Perhaps they were right. Yet some stiff-necked feeling in her could not agree.

"You know what?" Jean said. "I'm going to Ruth Benson and tell her the facts, myself."

"Oh, no!"

'Oh, yes. You darling zany."

"And now we have to run, dear," Charmion apologized. "We're going out on flights. Not ladies of leisure, as you are this week."

"I may be flying out myself," Vicki said forlornly. "May be going to Slick Pond soon, with Dean."

With Jean and Charmion gone, and the apartment empty once more, Vicki did not enjoy her involuntary leisure. She caught up on a number of chores—letters, mending, laundering, and practically renovating herself—but it was not much fun.

"I'll go out for lunch," she decided. "Broke or not. I'll get all dressed up, too. For morale."

She lunched in solitary grandeur at a famous restaurant. It was wonderful and it helped—for a while. Actually, Vicki spent a long, tiresome day: nothing happened until late that afternoon, when Vicki returned to the apartment.

"Two telegrams for ye," Mrs. Duff said. "One came collect."

Vicki ripped one open. It was signed "Carter Purnell," and read: "Joan has vanished again. Do you know where she might be? Please reply at once. We are frantic."

"Poor Mr. and Mrs. Purnell!" Vicki thought. She felt a little exasperated with Joan, and alarmed for her, too. The collect wire was from Joan, from Slick Pond:

"Stranded here. Address Commercial House. Not accomplishing a thing. Can you come? Need help. Joan."

"Oh, that foolish girl!" Vicki picked up the phone and dialed the telegraph office. "Even if she was upset, she should have used better judgment. . . . Hello! I want to send two telegrams, please."

One telegram went to Mr. and Mrs. Purnell, advising them Joan was in Slick Pond, and that Vicki would go down after her at once, to send her home. Vicki figured on going without Dean, if necessary. The other telegram went to Joan: "Coming immediately. Wait there. Vicki."

Then Vicki telephoned Dean. It took several calls, to the airport office, to the hangar, and finally to the Aviation Research Laboratory before Vicki could locate him.

"Hello," Dean said. "Feeling better, youngster? That's the stuff. . . . Yes, I'm free to leave New York, was just going to let you know. . . . Any time you say, now. I'm off until next Monday night. . . . Yes, I'm perfectly willing to go. I've been wanting to get home to Charleston for a day, anyhow. . . . She what? Joan what? . . . Well, of all the pointless things to do! . . . All right, we'll start tomorrow morning. . . . As early as you can make it. Five-thirty? . . . Right. Meet me in the lobby of the Administration Building. . . . My Piper Cub's in the

Norfolk hangar. We'll fly to Norfolk as ordinary passengers. . . . Wear warm clothes tomorrow, Vic. And
get yourself a good night's sleep tonight."

"Thank you, thank you, Dean! You're a real pal."

'So are you. So long."

At five-thirty of a bleak December morning, Vicki
and Dean met in the airport lobby, on Long Island.

Vicki was tense with excitement. She was bundled
up in her big overcoat, mittens, and a hood tied under
her chin. It would be cold flying in the Piper Cub.
Dean, towering beside her in a leather jacket and
heavy trousers and boots, looked over a flight map of
the southeastern states.

"You wait here, Vic. I'm going up to the Meteorologists' Room and ask 'em for a weather report. Our Norfolk plane doesn't leave for a little while yet. Go get
yourself a cup of coffee."

Dean Fletcher strode off, and Vicki obediently went
into the coffee shop. She had been seated a few minutes at the busy counter when Pete Carmody sat down
on the next stool.

"Morning, yellow-top. Where're you going, *out* of
flight uniform?"

"Hi, Pete. I'm hopping down to North Carolina, if
you must know."

"Who's flying you? Dean Fletcher, I suppose?"

"Mm-hmm. Have a piece of toast. What are you doing out here so bright and early?"

Pete shoved his hat back on his head. "Oh, I have to meet a plane with three celebrities aboard, and write 'em up. No, no toast! Tell me, instead, how'd Jean like the book I sent her?"

"Oho, so you're plying her with books, are you? And she didn't even tell us! What was the book about?"

Pete buried his face in his coffee cup. "Love sonnets."

Vicki giggled. "Jean will probably reciprocate with a book on aerodynamics."

Dean Fletcher burst into the coffee shop just then, looking for Vicki.

"Ready? Make it snappy. Hello, Carmody."

"Greetings. You look like one of the Rover Boys in that Great Outdoors outfit."

"You in that lit'ry hat," Dean kidded back. "Well, Vic, the weather's with us. Finished your coffee? Then let's go. So long, Pete. See you."

Vicki hastily gathered up her mittens and purse, and stood up. "All ready. Wish us luck, Pete."

"Good luck—and I wish you could talk Jean out of trying for that Mexico assignment." Pete reached for his notebook and grinned. "Tell Jean I'm much nicer than Mexico any day."

The trip south was uneventful. Aloft as passengers, they mapped out their route, marking Dean's flight map and using also the map of the Purnell timber tract which Joan had sent Vicki. They also discussed, uneasily, how they were going to persuade Joan to go home—and what they were going to say to Jim Badger.

"Providing we can find him," Vicki said, as the port of Norfolk hove into view.

"We'll find Badger, all right," Dean said a little grimly. "Guess I didn't tell you. I own a jeep—used to drive one of those tough little jobs occasionally when I was in the Army Air Forces. Wired my brother Bud, right after you phoned me, to drive it up to Slick Pond and leave it there for us. We'll use the jeep to go way back in the woods."

"We're flying straight to Slick Pond, then?"

"Right. After that, Charleston. To investigate there."

Landing at Norfolk, they hurried to the hangar where the small red plane waited. Now their journey began in earnest. Dean fueled Marietta, gave her engine a last-minute checkup, dragged her out on the airstrip, and he and Vicki crawled into the two seats. A mechanic spun the miniature propeller for them. Nothing happened.

Marietta refused to budge. Dean clambered out, tinkered frantically, called over two other pilots for a look.

"Try turning on your ignition," one of them suggested dryly.

Dean flushed. "So excited, I forgot," he muttered to Vicki, and clambered back in. "Come on now, Marietta. There's a good girl."

The little plane hummed, rolled obediently along the airstrip, and, skittish as a mosquito, soared up into the air. They were on their way.

It was still early in the morning as they flew over the farms of Virginia. Dean, calling back over his shoulder, estimated it would take them three hours, or maybe four, to reach Slick Pond. For one thing, the Piper Cub did not make much speed. For another, they were heading away from the coast and into the sandy wooded interior of North Carolina.

"Hope we don't run into fog," Dean called. "Hey, Vic, read this flight map and keep me on course, will you?"

Vicki, bouncing around in the back seat, closely followed the map and the landmarks below them. She had to keep on the alert. There were few of the white threads that meant highways, few towns through here, occasional blue chips of lakes: all seemed to be rolling woods, endless, silent, lonely. Dean flew with skill but alarmingly low. More than once Vicki saw their wings almost brush the branches, leaving them swaying as the plane passed.

Once she called forward, "Are we a plane or a lawn mower?"

Dean obligingly gained altitude, but he said, "Thought you'd want to study the timber."

She did: she needed to refresh her memory with the

sight of pine, hickory, ash, cypress, and gum. Soon they would be over the Purnell timber tract, and she wanted to be able to identify the trees growing there. So Vicki concentrated both on following their course, to guide Dean, and on these quiet stretches of forest.

It was an intensely interesting flight for Vicki, despite her worries about Joan Purnell, for she understood what she was seeing. These were not just trees, but future houses and ships. This was not just land, but a nation's natural resource, valuable, perishable, a potential help or a potential lack for the thousands of people who need things made of wood. These tracts belonged to someone—some owner like Joan's father whose family's fortunes depended on this timber.

"I sure am curious," Dean called back, "to meet this Jim Badger."

"So am I, Dean! And a little uneasy. Wonder what he's like?"

"Well, we'll soon find out. Watch our course."

Vicki resumed her vigil, looking down, looking at the flight map, looking down again. She saw cleared areas where timber had been logged out and only stumps stood; she saw tracts which had been partly cut over, and tracts which were virgin forest. Here and there, at the edge of rivers, they flew over lumber mills.

Once Vicki saw railroad tracks deep in the woods

and an engine, puffing white smoke, dragging a load of logs out of the forest. She saw trees being felled and then, a little later, several planes.

"What planes are those?" she called up to Dean.

"Forest Service, to detect fires, remember? Getting hungry, Vic?"

"A little. A little stiff and cold, too."

"We're almost there. Think Slick Pond will get out a brass band to greet us?"

Slick Pond was a fair-sized mill town. From the air they saw, clustered around it, villages in the fertile river valley. There was a river which cut through Slick Pond and lost itself in dense forests. Vicki and Dean landed in a farmer's field. Then they walked back to town along the highway, which turned into Slick Pond's main street. Everywhere there were long vistas of hills, shabby frame houses, hard-working people.

They picked up a timetable at the railroad station, then headed at once for the Commercial House. This was a small, old-time hotel for commercial travelers. In its seedy lobby they found Joan, looking pinched and forlorn.

"Vicki! And Dean too. Blessings on you both for coming to my rescue."

Vicki refrained from scolding the girl for the moment. Joan admitted she was hungry. Dean took one

skeptical look at the dining room here, and told both
girls to follow him. He hunted up a diner. They went
in and took a booth.

Dean ordered hearty lunches for them all. Joan ate
as if she was half starved. Only when Joan looked a
little brighter and less frightened did Vicki prod her
to talk.

"Well, I admit I did a foolish thing," Joan said. "I
was so sure I could unearth the facts here in Slick
Pond. But although I've been here since Tuesday afternoon and this is Thursday noon, I haven't learned
anything." Joan went on manfully. "I can't find Jim
Badger—don't know whether he's evading me or
whether he really is back in the woods logging all the
time, as the townspeople say. To get back in the woods
I'd need a car and that means hiring one, or a taxi, and
—well, my money has run out. I didn't realize train
fares and hotels and meals were going to be so expensive." Joan smiled sheepishly. "And I'd planned to
go on to Charleston, too."

"The only place you're going," Vicki said gently, "is
home."

"But I want to stay, now that you and Dean are
here!" Joan wailed. "You're going to hunt up Jim
Badger, aren't you? Why can't I come along?"

"Because you've caused your poor parents enough
worry already. Promise me that you'll never run away

again! No, Joanie, you're starting for home on the Norfolk train in— When does it leave, Dean?"

Dean looked at a timetable. "In exactly forty minutes."

Joan protested but finally, shamefaced, she gave in. Vicki soothed her, and Dean promised the girl that they would do their best to unravel her puzzle here in Slick Pond for her. Joan was placated. Vicki paid her hotel bill, bought a train ticket for her, put money in the girl's purse, and saw her safely on the train.

"Get in touch with me soon!" Joan called.

"As soon as we have news for you!" Vicki called back, waving. She and Dean stood on the platform and watched the train pull out, heading north.

CHAPTER XII

Mystery in the Forest

"WHEW!" SAID DEAN. "I'M GLAD JOAN'S TAKEN CARE OF.
Now let's pick up my jeep."

"Just a minute—I want to wire Mr. Purnell that Joan
is on her way." Vicki found a telegraph agent in the
station. "All ready now, Dean."

Dean located the garage where Bud had left his
jeep. Next they asked directions. No one in town, not
even the lumberjacks, were familiar with the name
Purnell. But they all knew Jim Badger.

"His stand's way back near the river, son. Take the
paved highway for 'bout two miles, then hit the first
big dirt road. From there on you'll have to ask your
way. That your jeep? Mighty fine jeep."

"Jim Badger expectin' you kids?" a logger asked.

"No," Vicki said, startled. "Why?"

"Jest that you'll have a time findin' anybody way
back in the wilderness. Nice feller, Jim. Everybody
likes Jim Badger."

Dean's jeep roared off down the highway. Vicki, despite her curiosity, felt uneasy. She wondered about Jim Badger, how to question him without making an enemy of him, who and what he was. Dean turned onto the dirt road and they bounced a good deal.

"Know what he looks like, Vic?"

"Vaguely. Not sure even of that," she said faintly.

"Say, where does this excuse for a road lead to?"

Dean maneuvered the sturdy jeep along the rutted yellow road, sideswiping low-hanging trees. They bumped along until the path ended altogether, at the edge of a forest. But they heard voices and the creak of machinery up ahead, so Dean drove on, slowly, between tree trunks. It was fragrant and half dark here in the woods, with a coolness and stillness that stirred Vicki.

"Must be right," Dean muttered. "There's a trail."

"I hear a river," Vicki said, "up ahead."

The jeep slowly pushed and nosed forward. Now and then they passed teams of lumberjacks felling trees. Once a small boy and his dog darted out toward them. It was hard, slow going until they got onto the woods road. Presently the sheds of a lumber mill, and a big lumberyard, came into view at a clearing. A red sports car was parked there.

"Badger's car, I'll bet," Dean said, over the sound of water and buzz saws. He drove the jeep up behind the red car. braked, and he and Vicki got out. They picked their way among piles of sawed boards, cranes, trucks, and workmen, and walked directly to the first shed. There was a man standing there, in checked flannel shirt and rough work pants, reading over a sheaf of papers. Dean said to him:

"Can you tell us where we can find Jim Badger?"

The man turned around. "I'm Jim Badger," he said, and smiled at them.

He was a hearty, outdoor man, heavy set, with a hail-fellow-well-met air. A shock of hair tumbled over his forehead like a boy's, and his ruddy face and light-blue eyes had a boy's candor. Vicki had to look again to realize that his sandy hair was streaked with gray.

"What can I do for you? Don't think I know you folks, but seems you know me, and I'm always glad to have callers. Gets pretty lonesome back here in the woods."

"I'm Vicki Barr, and this is Dean Fletcher," Vicki said. "We're friends of the Purnells."

His face changed ever so slightly, just for an instant, but the smile remained. "Oh, sure! My partner. Nice old codger, isn't he? Come on over on the sunny side of the shed. There's a bench there and we can sit down and talk. I want to hear all about how Purnell is, and how he's making out. How's his family?"

Affably smiling, Jim Badger led the way. If he wondered about or resented his partner's sending unexpected visitors down here, he gave no sign. They settled themselves on the bench, and Vicki said, as pleasantly as she could:

"I hope you don't mind our dropping in on you, Mr. Badger. Dean and I are on our way to Charleston, and since Mr. Purnell can't seem to reach you—"

"Sure, sure," he interrupted her, with a wave of his hand. "I've received his wires—my Charleston office sent 'em up to Slick Pond. You tell him I'm writing him a good, long letter right away. How is he?"

"Well, but worried. You're sending the shipments so fast, he says, and the freight charges are so high."

Jim Badger thumped his knee and laughed. "Now, isn't that just like Carter? Here we're doing a land-office business and he complains about it! Wants to slow the business down! You know, Miss Barr, Purnell is just no businessman. Can't grasp it. I'm awfully fond of him, but I wish he'd stick to his birds and bees!" Jim shook his head indulgently.

Vicki felt it was too soon to ask any direct questions of Jim Badger. She chatted along, trying to build up an acquaintance. Dean took part in the conversation, which swung from the natural beauties and wealth of this region to the lumber business. Jim Badger volunteered the information that he had been born and raised in this part of the country, had started out humbly as a lumberjack, had switched to the business end from the laboring end of the industry—"use my brains instead of my brawn." Slowly pulling himself up by his own bootstraps, he had achieved the job of assistant mill foreman, and then foreman, and had worked in that role for many years. Now, in middle age, Jim finally had won some ownership of the industry in which he had struggled so long.

"Local boy makes good," he chuckled. "In a small way. I still have ambitions to do better. Say, have you ever been through a lumber mill? Come on, I'll take you through, and explain how lumbering works." He added shrewdly to Vicki, "I s'pose you'll want to tell Carter all about this visit, when you get back."

Vicki was taken aback, and did not know what to reply.

Dean calmly threw back the challenge for her. "That's right, Badger, we'd like to learn all we can. You haven't any objections, have you?"

"Not an objection for miles around," Jim said cheerfully. "Glad to tell you anything you or Purnell would like to know. Well, this first shed here—"

They started to move through the mill. Vicki liked the fresh clean smell of pine trees being sawed into boards, and the sight of men busy at essential work. Jim explained that teams of lumberjacks cut down the trees, then the logs were floated downriver to the mill. Sometimes they had to use a train, or build river rafts, to drag the huge logs from the forest to the mill. "Some of these trees," Jim said with affection, "weigh one to three tons apiece. River's best. Washes off the sandy soil that clings after we drag the logs through the clearings. Sand would ruin our mill machinery."

Here at the sawmill, the timber was sawed, resawed, crosscut, and matched into various shapes and sizes for commercial use. Jim showed them squares, boards, sides, in the steam-filled planing mill; these were almost ready to be loaded on the railroad and shipped up to Norfolk. Jim mentioned shipping, markets and prices, the way clearing forests opens the land for agriculture. Vicki was impressed with Jim Badger's thorough knowledge. It compared favorably with her remembered talk with Gordon McQurg. It was obvious that Jim ran this lumber plant with an experienced hand.

The telephone rang. Jim Badger excused himself, and left Vicki and Dean standing alone.

"He certainly knows every angle of lumbering," Dean remarked. "He seems to know the commercial end of it as well as the forestry."

"No wonder Mr. Purnell needs him. Oh! Why, that's strange."

"What's strange, Vic?"

"Joan said Jim had no telephone back here in the woods. She and her father have been phoning Jim at the Charleston office and they're always told he's out logging. But there *is* a phone here."

Jim Badger came hurrying back, smiling, brushing back his shock of hair.

"Sorry. That was my Charleston office. Let's go outside. Too noisy in here."

They returned to the bench in the sun. Vicki sat tense, thinking of that telephone, thinking, too, that she could not put off her point-blank questions any longer.

"This is all extremely interesting," Vicki began. "I hope we're not taking too much time from your work. But I think the Purnells will be glad to know I've seen you."

"Good idea to drop by," Jim said good-naturedly. "Doggone Carter, I love him, but he's practically useless in this business. Always pestering me about one fool thing or another—because he doesn't understand head nor tail about lumbering. He just doesn't appreciate the difficulties I'm up against. I s'pose the professor's got a list of questions on his mind, as usual. You go right ahead, Miss Barr." He grinned and rested his head on his work-roughened hands.

Dean grinned a little in sympathy. "I suppose Purnell gets in your way?"

"He sure does! To tell you the truth, I'm trying to do his work, and mine too. And he only balls things up worse. Especially since our clerk, Miss Spry, left. Oh, well. He's a fine, scholarly old boy, and I know he thinks he's helping me. Go ahead, Miss Barr, shoot."

Vicki found it rather difficult, after Jim's bid for sympathy, and Dean's taking his side. Jim did make Purnell and his fears look foolish.

But her loyalties were with Mr. Purnell and Joan. Besides, Vicki reminded herself, all she knew about Jim Badger was what he chose to tell her. She drew a deep breath and said, "Mr. Purnell doesn't understand why you are routing the lumber up to Norfolk in such a long, roundabout way."

Simple, Jim replied with a laugh. What Purnell saw on paper—on the railroad timetables and maps— hardly told the actual, on-the-spot story. On paper, the Atlantic Coast Line Railroad route appeared direct, but it meant switching from the main line at Pembroke and then back to the main line at Rocky Mountain, and that meant extra switching charges. So that was out. There was, Jim said, a quite direct route on the Seaboard Air Line Railway and Connections. But this line had a tie-up with planes and bus lines, ran tours, and Jim felt it was for travelers, not for shipping. That left only the Southern Railway System, with its roundabout route from Slick Pond, and that was the one Jim used. It sounded plausible.

Vicki could not quite believe Jim's reasons. Switching? But Jim's route involved switching, too, and backtracking besides. Tourists? Irrelevant; cargo was a

separate matter. She thought of the twenty-five-thousand-dollar freight bill Jim ran up and asked:

"Does your railroad agent approve of your routing?"

"Ganner? Sure he approves. Ganner's an old pal of
mine. I use his Southern Railway to ship to Charleston,
too"—Jim caught himself, flushed unaccountably, and
hurried on—"I do all my shipping by the same road, so
Ganner and I work together pretty efficiently by this
time. Ganner doesn't have to stop and question my
routing every time I send a load of lumber. He knows
I know my business," he added, rather indignantly.

"No offense," Vicki murmured, but she was not convinced. From everything McQurg had told her, she
still thought Jim's routing unnecessarily extravagant.
"Another thing that's worrying Mr. Purnell—if you
don't mind more questions? He says you are shipping
the lumber up to Norfolk so fast that you're running
him into debt. I understand there was a twenty-five
thousand dollar freight bill, recently."

"For Pete's sake!" Then Jim burst out laughing. "If
that isn't just like Carter! What does he want me to
do, keep the lumber here in the woods and turn down
buyers' orders? Of course I have to ship it fast—I have
to send it when the buyers want it! Can't tell 'em 'Wait
a couple of months, boys.' They wouldn't buy."

Dean muttered his agreement.

But Vicki said gravely, "Maybe you could space the

shipments. At any rate, you've put Mr. Purnell in an awfully difficult position."

Jim's eyes popped wide open in concern. "Well, gosh, I didn't mean to hurt him in any way. You mean he can't raise the twenty-five thousand?"

There was something hungry in his eyes and voice that made Vicki uneasy. She hoped she had not exposed to this ambitious man exactly how weak Mr. Purnell's position was.

"You mean Purnell can't raise the twenty-five thousand?" Jim Badger asked again.

Vicki glanced down. "I don't really know."

"But you ought to know."

Leaning toward her, and changing his tone, Jim said smoothly, and Vicki recognized that he was still probing:

"Even if Carter hasn't that amount in his pocket, he could easily discount the bills of lading at the bank. Or," Jim said, suddenly pouncing, "has the bank refused him a long-term loan?"

Vicki held firm. "I don't know, Mr. Badger. I'm sorry, but I simply don't know."

Dean looked guardedly from one to the other, alert to this battle of wits.

Jim straightened up. "There's only one bank in Norfolk that Purnell does business with. I suppose the others would think there was something fishy if he asked them to extend twenty-five thousand dollars on a single deal."

"Do you know them?" Vicki asked, careful to sound casual and not to mention the Roland name.

"No, I don't know the Norfolk banks. Well, say, I'm sorry if old Carter is in any trouble. Hard on a nervous man like him. Tell him not to worry. Tell him," Jim said warmly, "we've got huge orders, orders pouring in all the time—tell him everything will be fine, just to leave it to me—"

"That reminds me." Vicki made another effort. "It's hard to understand why you ship only pine up to Norfolk, and never any of the valuable ash and hickory."

Jim Badger's ruddy face became humorously resigned. "*What* ash and hickory? Now look here, Miss Barr." He patted her arm. "You go back and tell Carter from me to quit imagining things, and just leave everything to his partner, Jim Badger. I know this business inside out, and I promise you, Purnell hasn't a thing in the world to worry about."

Their interview was over. Jim strolled to the parked jeep with them, and admired it. He said the red car was his, and showed Dean the mileage he had rolled up on it. They all shook hands, and Jim, with a satisfied look, said cordially:

"Stop in again on your way back, if you can make it. Always glad to see you. Well, so long!"

Dean drove the jeep along the woods road. Vicki sat beside him in silence. Not until they had entered the forest, winding slowly along a trail, did she speak.

"Dean, what do you think of him?"

Dean rubbed his lean jaw. "Seems like a good boy. But he talks too much."

"Yes. He talks a lot and tells nothing. Funny, his telling strangers like us his life history. It sounded rehearsed to me. As if—as if he wanted to be sure people've got exactly the right impression of him. He painted a nice, sympathetic picture of himself."

Dean grunted. "Kind of suspicious, aren't you?"

"Well, it *is* funny about that telephone. Also, what is he shipping to Charleston? Joan said all the shipping is done out of Norfolk, by her father. And I still wonder whether there's ash and hickory, or not."

"We'll go up and see," Dean said tersely.

"Do we have to do it this minute? I'd like to have a breather. That interview wasn't very pleasant, even if Jim Badger did smile constantly."

Dean looked at his wrist watch. He said they ought to get back to the plane, and get up, while there was still plenty of daylight to see Purnell's tract, and to fly the hundred miles down to Charleston. But Dean agreed that there was enough time for them to drive around a bit.

"Let's climb a hill, for a view," Vicki suggested.

The jeep, clinging like a caterpillar, chugged along

merrily. Vicki hung onto its side as they started up a low hill. Gradually the dense growth of trees thinned out, and instead of branches for a roof, open sky appeared overhead.

At the top of the hill perched a trim cabin, with a platform built around its four sides. Pacing it was a young man in sturdy khaki breeches and shirt, and broad-brimmed hat; he looked through binoculars out over the wooded miles. A horse, tethered to a tree, arched its neck and nuzzled the thin grass. It was so still here, the wind blew like music.

"Hallo!" Dean called. "Hallo!"

The young man turned around, silhouetted against the blue sky. He saw them and waved. "Hello, there! Come up and talk!"

Vicki and Dean scrambled out of the jeep and up to the cabin. The young man gave Vicki a hand up onto the platform. She saw his browned face, his erect carriage like a horseman's.

He was a forest ranger, and this was a ranger station. His days and nights were spent here, in this lonely spot, on the lookout to detect forest fires. Other rangers were out on patrol, he explained—on horseback in the woods, in patrol planes over the woods.

"What a marvelous life," Dean said. "Always outdoors."

"But isn't it lonesome?" Vicki asked.

"Ma'am, if you loved the woods like I do, you

wouldn't ask that question. And if you understood the
danger of fire starting, and leaping from tree to tree,
and eating up whole miles of forests—then you'd understand why this is my lifework."

Vicki knew fire was a killer. But never until now had
she thought about what terror and forlorn waste could
be started by a campfire's embers not quite cold, or a
cigarette tossed from a car, or one small match dropped
on last autumn's leaf or dry grass and still glowing.
Flames could climb and sweep in minutes over trees
that were centuries in the growing, leaving charred
stumps and ashes, desolate untillable land, and burning to death the forest animals in a roaring sheet of
flame. As the forest ranger talked, saying nine out of
ten forest fires were man-made, and needless, Vicki
determined never to risk even the very smallest care-
lessness with fire in the woods.

"This is Smoky Bear," said the ranger, showing them
a poster on his cabin wall. Smoky Bear was a large,
plump, very worried-looking bear in trousers and hat,
exasperatedly pouring a bucket of water over a fire
some careless picnickers had not drowned and stirred
and drowned again.

"What do you do," Dean asked, "when a forest fire
actually does break out?"

"We try to spot fires before they can spread. We
try to check the source or start of the fires, and prevent
them beforehand. But if a fire does get started, with

the trees standing close together and the wind whipping the flames along, and few roads to get through —well— Have you heard of smoke jumpers?"

These daring men parachuted from Forest Service planes, with fire-fighting equipment loaded on their backs, and battled the conflagration alone, deep in the forests.

"Whew!" Dean exclaimed. "I'm a flier, but smoke jumper is one job I wouldn't care for."

"Let's hope there won't be any forest fires," Vicki murmured. This visit, in this lonely spot, had impressed her very much.

They said good-bye to the ranger, and turned the jeep downhill once more. It took them half an hour to drive back to Slick Pond, and then park the jeep in the garage. Dean said they had better hurry, if they were to fly by daylight. They hiked back as fast as they could to the farmer's field and the waiting red plane. Afternoon shadows were lengthening around the town's mills, along the highway, under Marietta's wing.

Dean managed an abrupt take-off in the cramped field, and up they went. Vicki got out the Purnell map. What had been thirty minutes' hard driving was a very few minutes in the air. Soon they were over the Purnell timber tract; there stood the mill sheds below, that red blob was Jim Badger's car, there ran the river.

Vicki checked directions and exact tract boundaries

by map and compass, and then called to Dean:

"All right, now go down as low as you dare."

The little plane dipped. Dean flew the Piper Cub so slowly that she made a good deal of noise.

"This all right, Vic?" he shouted back.

"Fine! Keep going, and turn when I tell you!"

Vicki leaned out and watched sharply. They almost grazed tops of trees bearing yellow cones. That was pine. There were extensive logged-out areas here in the pine stand. Vicki could see the stumps of the trees that had been felled.

But what was this they were coming to?

"Turn east!"

Marietta obediently turned, and then dropped low. They flew over other trees now. These shot straight up without branches in the confine of the forest, but with spreading branches at their very tops. That form, and their bark, belonged unmistakably to a nut tree. Hickory!

"Fly over and over this stand, will you?"

Yes, there was hickory, as Joan and her father had supposed and as Jim Badger had denied. Valuable hickory! Vicki saw a few cleared areas: the hickory had been partly logged out. Vicki got out a pencil and diagrammed the area.

And now they floated over tall, massive trees, trees conspicuous for their grayish twigs and black buds. This was ash, and the most valuable of all. Here was another stand Jim Badger had lied about. The ash, too, had been partly logged out.

"There *is* hickory and ash! Some of it's been cut over! Jim showed us stockpiles of cut lumber, but he showed us only cheap yellow pine. What's become of the cut ash and hickory? Why has Mr. Purnell never received anything from Jim Badger but low-grade pine? Dean!" she shouted. "Do you realize what we've just seen?"

He nodded. They had seen proof incontrovertible that Jim Badger was dishonest, and obviously involved in some unscrupulous scheme.

Then, over near the riverbank, but concealed in the edge of the forest, they saw one more thing. Timber cut into squares was being loaded onto a backed-up freight train. But the timber was not the pine Jim had pointed out to them in the mill, and the train was not headed for Norfolk. Dean said that train was headed for Charleston.

As they flew on to Charleston in the fading daylight, Vicki's heart was heavy.

CHAPTER XIII

Stranger's Warning

VICKI WAS NOT A VERY SATISFACTORY GUEST AT THE Fletchers'. She felt guilty at not having brought Dean's mother a hostess gift, at failing Howdy and Chips in their desire to play cops and robbers, at dodging stern Mr. Fletcher's engineering disquisitions. But the Fletchers, who had heard from Dean about the Purnell family's troubles, told Vicki not to stand on ceremony, but to go ahead with her urgent business.

Vicki's concern here in Charleston was to trace that hickory and ash, and to find out anything else she could about Jim Badger. Dean's father had kindly supplied her with introductions to lumbermen, a freight agency, and exporters, where she might make inquiries. In particular, Mr. Fletcher had telephoned a Mr. Cargill in Vicki's behalf. She started out early in the morning, walking through the stately and beautiful city.

She wished she was going this mild morning to visit the Magnolia Gardens, up the Ashley, or to see

a Tudor mansion at the Middleton place, farther up
the river. Instead, she trotted down to the water-front
district and located the business street where shippers
and lumbermen had their offices.

In the marble lobby of the first building she entered,
Vicki stopped for a moment in a corner, to screw up
courage. She was hardly in the habit of walking into
business offices and requesting more or less confidential
information, even though Dean's father had vouched
for her. But Dean said it was perfectly usual to ask to
see the top men and state frankly what she wanted to
know. Dean assured her that she would find businessmen easy to approach and willing to help.

"Maybe businessmen exchange information all the
time," Vicki thought, "but I don't even *look* like a businessman!" She wished she was dressed in something
more prepossessing and morale building than the sports
clothes she had flown down in.

She marched determinedly into one of the elevators,
ascended to the seventh floor, and entered the offices
marked WATSON, CARGILL, & THOMAS, SHIPPERS' LINE.

The receptionist must have been surprised to see
a small girl, in hood and suit, asking to see the presi-
dent.

"Are you expected? Will you state your business?"

"I believe Mr. Cargill expects me. Mr. Fletcher
phoned for an appointment for me."

The receptionist invited her to be seated and went

into Mr. Cargill's office. In a few minutes she reappeared, holding a door open.

"Mr. Cargill will see you. The office on your left."

Vicki's knees stopped quaking the moment she saw the pleasant, middle-aged man behind the desk. He rose to greet her, gave her a chair, resumed his own, and said comfortably:

"Very well, Miss Barr, I'm at your service."

"Mr. Cargill, I am in Charleston in the interests of Mr. Carter Purnell, Jim Badger's partner. They own a lumber business in Slick Pond."

Mr. Cargill nodded. "I know Jim Badger well. He does some of his foreign shipping through our company." Vicki was puzzled: Joan had distinctly said all the shipping was done through Norfolk, through Mr. Purnell. Mr. Cargill went on, "We're the biggest shippers down here, we handle almost all the lumber export out of Charleston. I was aware Jim must have a partner or an associate of some kind—Carter Purnell's name was in the newspaper when Clayton Purnell's will was probated. I was interested," Mr. Cargill explained to Vicki, "because Clayton Purnell's family and mine have been friends for years. Though I never knew Carter Purnell, I feel a sympathy for any member of the Purnell family. Your Mr. Purnell inherited those tracts, wasn't that it?"

"Yes, sir, that's correct." Vicki briefly explained the

setup of the partnership, being careful neither to expose Purnell's unfortunate position nor to cast any slander on Jim Badger. "I'd like to ask you, Mr. Cargill, whether you ship any hickory and ash for Jim Badger."

Mr. Cargill looked at her oddly. Vicki realized he was studying her. Then he said:

"Since you represent Jim's partner, I see no reason not to tell you. Yes, Miss Barr, we do ship hickory and ash for Jim Badger. Down to South America—we Charleston shippers naturally handle the southern ocean routes. Jim ships to Rio de Janeiro—there's a ski industry down there, in the mountains, and also furniture factories which buy Jim's woods."

"It is Purnell's wood, too!" Vicki told herself.

"Mr. Cargill, could you—could you tell me a little more about your dealings with Jim Badger?"

He looked at her with a fatherly air. "Something worrying you, Miss Barr? I'm perfectly willing to tell you. So far as my firm is concerned, our business is open and aboveboard, and we don't deal in secrets. About Jim—" He cleared his throat. "As I understand it, Jim owns the ash and hickory tracts independently. Jim has indicated to me on several occasions that his South American business is separate from the business of the Purnell firm."

Vicki asked anxiously, "Mr. Cargill, do you think

Jim Badger is as trustworthy as Mr. Purnell seems to believe?"

"Certainly, certainly. Jim's a fine fellow."

In an agency which acted for all railways in this southern region, Vicki talked with a Mr. Purdue. Since he handled the services of all the railroads equally, Mr. Purdue could be counted on to be impartial. He agreed with Vicki that the route Jim used, to Norfolk, was wildly extravagant. He agreed, too, that Jim's reasons for not using the other, more direct, cheaper lines and routes were no reasons at all. In fact, Mr. Purdue was puzzled at running up such huge and unnecessary railroad bills. "Ganner must be getting careless," he remarked, "to let Jim Badger make such a costly error." Vicki thought unhappily, but did not say, "It is Mr. Purnell who has to pay for Jim's 'error.'"

In a second, smaller shipping house, to which Mr. Fletcher had provided her an introduction, Vicki was told the same thing Mr. Cargill had said. "Yes, we send hickory and ash to South America for Jim Badger." They showed her the books. The transactions were listed in the independent name of Jim Badger. The Purnell name appeared nowhere. This firm, too, had been told by Jim Badger that he owned the valuable ash and hickory independently of Purnell. It was believed Jim merely handled these tracts along with the tracts of the Purnell company.

"In fact," they said, "Jim Badger had told us that,

with the profits from his South American deals, he plans to buy out Purnell. That is common knowledge, Miss Barr."

Buy out or *push out* Purnell! Vicki trembled so violently that she could hardly speak. She thanked the shipping people and left, to stand on the sidewalk, stunned with what she had learned. Jim Badger was a cheat! A genial, likable cheat! Behind the easy smile, the warm friendly manner, the show of affection for "old Carter," Jim was coldly selfish, and crooked to the core.

Vicki wandered around the water-front streets, hardly seeing where she was going. She was too shocked and revolted to be able to think constructively yet. The cheek of Jim Badger! His maneuvers and ad-missions were made openly, boldly! He did not even bother to cover up his traces. With Miss Spry away, he probably thought his big chance had come.

Of course what Jim had counted on was that Mr. Purnell would never be distrustful enough or practical enough to come down here and investigate independ-ently, as Vicki was doing. Vicki realized now that part of Jim's plan was to keep his partner so busy in Norfolk, and in such trouble up there, that the harassed Purnell would have no opportunity to come down to Charles-ton to investigate.

"Jim must not have been at all pleased to have Dean and me show up yesterday," she thought wryly. "But he certainly put on a good show! Everything so open and aboveboard—even showed us through the mill! Volunteered information! Answered questions before I could ask them—to keep me from asking the wrong questions!"

Suddenly she stared at the plate-glass front of an office, and stopped. The window said, in old-fashioned gold letters: PURNELL LUMBER COMPANY. Above this, in newer and bigger letters than the originals, had been added JIM BADGER.

Should she go in? Vicki saw a man writing at a high bookkeeper's desk, and a girl typing. No, there was no point in going in. They would merely give her the same evasions they gave Mr. Purnell and Joan when they wired or telephoned long-distance from Norfolk. Besides, Jim's bookkeeper and secretary might warn Jim that a Miss Barr had been investigating him. Vicki did not want Jim Badger to know that just yet. She needed time in which to think out a plan to safeguard Joan's father.

Vicki trudged back to the Fletcher house. Lunch was long since past—she had lost track of the time, had forgotten to telephone Dean's mother that she would not be back for lunch. But Mrs. Fletcher forgave her and fed her and left her free to go on with the day's business. Dean telephoned from downtown and Vicki asked him if he would mind coming home. She had to talk to him.

"What did you learn, Vic?" he asked, a few minutes

later, as he came bounding up the porch steps three at a time.

"I learned," she said miserably, "that Jim Badger is selling Purnell's wood on the sly and pocketing the proceeds, and deliberately running up huge freight bills to ruin Mr. Purnell financially. It seems plain to me that Jim Badger has been planning to force Mr. Purnell out of the business, from the moment he inherited it and Jim wormed his way into a partnership!"

As Dean listened, his lean face hardened. "What are you going to do?"

"That's what I want to talk over with you, Dean. I have several ideas, but I don't think any of them are much good. I guess the first step is to let Mr. Purnell know what's going on. As soon as possible, so the Purnells can protect themselves from this—this—underhanded—"

Since a telegram giving all the facts would be much too long, they decided a long-distance telephone call was best. They went into the hallway, where the telephone was, and Vicki called the operator. She asked for Norfolk, Virginia, giving Mr. Purnell's name and telephone number.

"Sorry, all the lines to Norfolk are busy," operator said. "I'll keep trying, and I'll call you back when I reach your party."

"Midafternoon like this, the wires are always crowded," Dean explained.

They waited. The phone did not ring. After an

hour, the operator rang and said she now had a line to Norfolk. She put through Vicki's call but there was no answer at the Purnell house.

"Are you certain you're ringing the right number?" Vicki asked anxiously. "Are you sure their phone isn't out of order? This call is urgent."

Vicki could hear the distant phone ringing. It rang and rang and rang.

The operator said, "Your party doesn't answer, miss. Shall I keep trying? If your party answers, I'll ring you back."

Vicki agreed to that and wearily put down the telephone.

"Maybe we'd better send a telegram, Dean."

"Wait a little longer," he counseled. "We have to be here through dinner, anyhow, and it's nearly dinnertime now. Maybe your call will come through while we're at the table."

Vicki sat through dinner tensely, trying to keep her mind on the Fletchers' conversation, jumping when the telephone rang once. But the Norfolk call did not come. Dinner over, Dean said, "Come on, Vic. We've waited long enough. We'll go downtown and send that telegram."

They got their coats, for even here in the South the December evening was chilly. They started walking downtown, trying to compose the telegram on the way.

On their way to the telegraph office, Vicki and Dean

bumped into Mr. Cargill and his wife. They were getting out of their car. The middle-aged man hailed her, to Vicki's surprise, and the four people stopped on the crowded sidewalk.

"Miss Barr! Oh, Miss Barr! This is lucky—I was just about to telephone you at the Fletchers'."

"To telephone *me*, sir?"

Mr. Cargill said hastily, "Come into this drugstore. I have important news for you. This is Miss Barr, Mrs. Cargill, and you already know Dean."

They followed the businessman into the drugstore, and filed into a booth. Mr. Cargill ordered ice cream and waved the waitress away.

"Miss Barr," he said earnestly, leaning across the table in the bright drugstore lights, "I may be talking out of turn and you may not want to take a warning from a stranger. But you are a nice, honest child, and what's more, Clayton Purnell was a friend of my father's. I can't stand by and see any of the Purnells treated like this!"

"Like what?" Vicki breathed. Her heart seemed to stop beating, so slow were its beats of fear.

"Miss Barr, I've changed my mind about Jim Badger. He blew into town this afternoon. He found out that you were asking questions about him, and tracking down his—his—well, I wouldn't have believed this of him twelve hours ago—but I'm beginning to think that Badger's business dealings are open to question. I would never have believed that Jim could be anything but honest."

Vicki hesitated. "I suppose he's furious—with me?"

"Yes, he is. And I think Jim Badger is going to retaliate."

"How?" Dean demanded. "Did Jim give you any inkling?"

"He's too sharp to forewarn anyone. No," Mr. Cargill said, "I don't know how he'll strike. But he will. One more thing," he added slowly. "Jim also learned you two youngsters have a plane and that you flew over his tracts yesterday. I don't know why that burned him up so terribly, but it did. Now, I want you to keep this to yourselves, but I thought you ought to know."

Mr. Cargill and his wife left the drugstore.

Vicki was terribly upset.

"Dean, I have a hunch we ought to go back to Slick Pond first thing in the morning, and see Jim Badger again."

CHAPTER XIV

Fire!

———

VICKI AND DEAN WERE UP AT FIVE THE NEXT MORNING, and off in Marietta, in a sky just turning pink with sunrise.

They flew the hundred miles to Slick Pond, aided by favorable winds. They were eager to arrive as early as possible, for not a great deal of their free time was left. Both of them had to report back to New York on Monday. This was Saturday, and they still had unfinished business with Jim Badger.

Vicki did not know what to expect next. But Mr. Purnell's bewilderment and Joan's pitiful face rose up before her eyes and drove out any fear of Jim Badger.

The Cub buzzed steadily ahead. The sun rose, the pink glow strengthened then faded, the sky grew bluer. Below them, towns began to awaken and trucks and cars appeared on the white thread of highway. As they flew northward, the forests appeared.

When they drew near to Slick Pond, the sky became

rosy again. Vicki did not wonder at this, immersed as she was in guessing at Jim Badger's plans. But she saw Dean's back stiffen and his head turn in all directions.

"What's the matter, Dean?" she called.

"Studying the sky. Don't understand that pink glow straight ahead of us."

"The tail end of dawn, that's all."

"No," he said emphatically. "The pink covers too small and concentrated an area."

He urged Marietta on. The forests beneath them were beautiful to see. The freshness of early morning lay on the miles of woodland, as if all the earth had been newly created.

"It's darned funny," Dean shouted over the engine noise.

"What is?"

"That pink spot. See it? Over the crest of the hill, must be just a few miles beyond Slick Pond. And it's getting redder."

"I see smoke!" Vicki shouted. "Dean! That—that's fire!"

"In two minutes we'll be over Slick Pond and we'll see what it is."

When the town lay at their feet, it was peaceful in the blue shadow of early morning. No fire there. The red spot lay farther on, and it fanned out in the clear sky, billowing smoke.

"The woods are afire!"

"Dean!" Vicki's throat tightened as a miserable intuition struck her. "Fly on and see if it's—" She could not bring herself to say "the Purnell timber tract."

Dean forced the little airplane on. They passed over Slick Pond. Smoke drifted into their nostrils now, the pungent smoke of wood. Vicki got a throatful of it. The sky ahead glowed redder. Over the river they flew, and saw, below, the sheds of the Purnell-Badger mill. Then a flame licked a treetop ahead of them, and Vicki gasped.

"It's the Purnell tract that's on fire, all right!" Dean shouted at her.

A dozen disconnected thoughts rattled against one another in Vicki's tormented brain. Was this the hopeless end of Mr. Purnell's business, and the fruitless end of her efforts to help?

"Dean, would you dare fly over it? So we can see?"

Dean nodded and plunged the plane forward, right over the smoking area. The Cub rocked in the strong thermal currents caused by the fire. To be able to breathe in all this smoke, Vicki had to hold her handkerchief over her nose and mouth. Her eyes stung and watered, but she prodded Dean to keep going forward. They were taking a long chance: they both knew it. A drift of wind—an unexpected updraft of flame—and Marietta's gasoline tank would explode like a firecracker.

As they flew over the flaming area, they could see

the red-orange fire creep like a licking snake up trunk and branch, and consume the living trees. The scene had a livid and awful beauty.

"Dean—look!"

Vicki, looking down, had made a major discovery. The fire seemed to be radiating out from places partially logged out, as if fire had started in the bare spots. It did not make sense! Wouldn't a fire, starting accidentally, break out or at least quickly establish itself in the most thickly wooded stands? Or had the fire been deliberately set—thoughtfully set in partially logged-out areas where it would do a minimum of damage? And it was hickory and ash that were burning!

If Jim Badger wanted an alibi or a cover-up for having cut and sold hickory and ash to South America without his partner's knowledge, this forest fire certainly provided an excuse! Jim could plead the fire as a reason for Purnell to sell out quickly—without any investigation of the tract or of business records. Jim was taking a chance, with these valuable woods on fire, but most of this timber had been cut, anyway. A most convenient accident, if accident it was!

"Dean, go on! Go over the rest of the tract!"

Dean swerved the plane south over the river, and flew over other portions of the tract. The differentiated branches rose up under them, and Vicki hung out the

side of the plane, peering. The burning area was sur-
rounded by completely logged-out areas of the pine
stand—as if precautions had been taken against the
fire's spreading.

It was too much of a coincidence to believe that the
forest fire was an accident. Dean, yelling back unintel-
ligibly, had come to the same conclusion about Jim's
guilt.

"But just the same, Dean, Jim is taking a long
chance with the hickory and ash! Suppose the fire
spreads to the parts that haven't been logged out yet?"

"Vic, I want to do something providing it's okay
with you."

"What do you want to do?"

"I want to land and look around."

"That's exactly what I want myself!"

Dean had trouble getting down. He banked and
turned over the woods road, but had to go up again,
then spiral down again in a better spot on the road.
They touched ground with a jar, but safe. Before the
propeller had stopped spinning, Vicki and Dean
climbed out of the plane.

"Which way?"

"Can you stand breathing all the smoke, Vic?"

"Let's try it, anyhow."

They left the Piper Cub parked at one side of the
woods road, above the lumber mill, and started on

foot. Dean found an opening leading into the forest, crossed by many tire tracks, and they followed that trail.

They had not gone many yards when smoke began to curl toward them. They pushed on, Vicki coughing a little. The trail of tire tracks disappeared, the smoke grew thicker, and they seemed to have lost their bearings. They hesitated as to which way to turn.

Vicki saw a tongue of flame crazily leap up some distance ahead. "Let's go as close as we dare."

"All right. But we'll have to be quick." Dean held aside a low-hanging branch, for her to get past.

Breathing through their handkerchiefs now, they pushed deeper into the smoke-filled forest. Vicki stumbled over tree roots and happened to glance down.

"Dean! Here're some more car tracks!"

It was a double track, a new track, as if a car had gone in and come out again. In the moist soil, the arrow-shaped tire prints showed up fresh and clear. Dean stared at them.

"Vic. Hasn't Badger got arrow-patterned tires on that red car of his?"

"I—think so. Not certain." She coughed, and wiped the tears out of her stinging eyes. "Come on. Follow the tire tracks."

They joined hands and stumbled ahead, hurrying, choking.

"We'd better run," Dean gasped.

They ran, as best they could, feeling the heat now, and hearing the crackle of flames ahead. The arrow-shaped tire tracks led directly into the forest fire. Apparently the fire had started very close to here. They dared not go farther.

Then they both saw it at once. Nearly indistinguishable in the swirling gray smoke, a small, gray-brown object lay on the ground. It was a hat. Dean darted forward, snatched it, seized Vicki's hand, and they fled.

They fought their way back, located the regular trail again, and at last emerged onto the woods road. They were exhausted, breathing heavily. Their faces and hands were smudged, and their clothes smelled strongly of wood smoke.

"Have to rest," Vicki panted.

"Yep. Let's—sit down."

They sank down at the side of the road, and gulped in the cool, clean air. Now that the risk was past, Vicki trembled uncontrollably. She made herself breathe deeply, to calm down. When they could speak again, Dean examined the hat, which was seared as if a sudden flame had licked it.

"Look!" Dean exclaimed. "It has the initials J.B. on the inside band. I guess this clinches it."

"Hang onto that hat, Dean. It's valuable evidence."

"Don't I know it! That crook!"

Vicki felt as shocked and furious with Badger as

Dean did. But her mind was on the swift sibilant flames, hungrily eating up the Purnells' property.

"Dean, we'd better notify the Forest Service—in case the rangers haven't spotted it. There's a phone at the mill."

"Think Badger'll let us use his phone?" Dean asked sardonically. But he jumped up and helped Vicki to her feet. "If the Forest Service can only send smoke jumpers—in time—"

They hurried down the woods road, toward the mill and the telephone. Dean carried the hat they had found.

In a few minutes they caught sight of Jim Badger's red car up ahead, parked near the mill. Vicki gave a nervous start. She had not thought about the possibility of encountering Jim Badger here and now. But she understood why he had not run away from the scene of the fire. Guilty or not, Badger would be too clever to run away, for that would point suspicion to him.

Then, as they neared the mill and were nearly at the red car, they saw Jim Badger himself, his back to them. No one was around. Probably everyone else had gone to fight the fire.

Dean put a hand on Vicki's arm. He said in a low tone, "Wait a minute. I want to have a look at the tires on Badger's car."

They stopped in the road. Dean bent and examined

the tires. Their tread was arrow-patterned. Traces of forest soil still clung to them.

"What d'you think you're doing around my car?"

It was Jim Badger, shouting at them. He strode rapidly down the road, waving his arm.

"What are you two kids doing around here, anyhow?"

Dean waited until Jim came closer. Then the flier said calmly:

"Any objections to our being around here?"

"You're on my property! Say, did you see the fire?" Jim Badger's tone had changed quickly. "Isn't this terrible? A lifetime of work going up in smoke!"

Vicki ventured to ask, "Did—did anybody notify the Forest Service yet?"

"Why, sure. I did!" Jim exclaimed. "Just now. Just got through phoning them. The rangers had spotted it, of course—but their plane station with the smoke jumpers is a long ways from Slick Pond. Tract can be ruined before they get here. I'm just sick—"

"You really phoned the Forest Service?" Dean repeated skeptically. Vicki, too, wondered if Jim Badger was telling the truth.

"What do you mean, did I really phone them? Do you think I *want* to lose my timber? Look, fellow, you can go phone 'em and notify 'em yourself—in case you think I'm crazy or something," Jim said aggrievedly,

He ran his hand through his shock of hair. "If you know any way to get those fire fighters here faster, I'll thank you for it!"

Vicki wavered. Jim certainly seemed upset about the fire. Then Jim saw the hat in Dean's hand. His jaw tensed.

"Where'd you find that hat?" he demanded.

"Farther up," Dean said noncommittally. "Why? Is it yours?"

For a fraction of a second, Badger hesitated. "Looks like my hat. Let me see it." Badger held out his hand.

Dean did not hand the hat over. Instead, he turned it so that Jim could see his own initials in the inner band. He looked at Jim with his usual quiet, steady gaze. "Yours?"

"Yeah. I—uh—lost it—the other day. Don't know just where—I was out logging," Jim explained. "Where'd you find it, Fletcher?"

"Just up there a piece."

"You find it in the woods?"

"Thought you didn't know where you lost it."

"In the woods?" Badger repeated. "Where in the woods?"

The man's tone made Vicki shrink back.

"And why were you looking at the tires on my car? *Give me that hat!*"

The two men faced each other tensely, Badger ready to spring. Dean said:

peatedly on the back of Jim's head. But the older man's weight was telling. He brought his knee up, driving it into Dean's side. The pilot gritted his teeth and gave a convulsive heave that threw Jim away from him. Jim scrambled back, his powerful arms reaching. Dean landed a punch that tore open Badger's cheek.

Vicki screamed again, for help. But there was no one to answer. She saw Jim's big hands lock around Dean's throat.

She started forward and her foot kicked a good-sized rock. She bent swiftly and picked it up, then tried to get close to the struggling men. Dean's face was purple, but he was still fighting, trying to break the older man's hold. As Vicki ran up, the pilot suddenly clapped his hands over Badger's ears, a painful, ear-shattering blow that made Jim roar again and relax his hold.

Instantly Dean was on his feet. He saw Vicki, and his outflung arm pushed her away. She backed up and dropped the rock. Dean didn't want her help.

A plane roared overhead. On its underwing, Vicki made out the insignia of the Forest Service. She ripped off her jacket, waving it and yelling.

Dean was fighting with more caution now, respecting Jim's superior weight and skill at infighting. He boxed, keeping out of Jim's reach, landing repeated punches. Jim kept boring in, taking Dean's blows, intent on getting his hands on the pilot again.

Dean set himself for a hard right to the jaw—and

Badger stamped his heavy shoe on the pilot's instep!

The trick threw Dean off balance, ruined the timing of the blow. Jim avoided it, and, his foot still locking Dean's, he lifted his arm in a sizzling uppercut that landed with a sickening thump on the side of Dean's face.

Dean buckled, his knees unhinged by the terrific blow. It was the advantage Jim needed. He rushed in, his shoulder catching Dean in the stomach. Both of them went down. Jim straddled Dean, his knees pressing into the pilot's stomach. With his powerful hands he gripped the helpless boy's shoulders and began methodically pounding his head against the ground.

Dean's body was limp now. With a little sob Vicki picked up the rock again and tried to hit Jim. He reached out and pushed her away, so hard that she almost fell.

But the Forest Service plane was coming down!

Vicki ran to it as the pilot swooped low over the road, fishtailing to kill his speed. In a moment the pilot jumped out. "What's the matter?"

"Stop them," Vicki pleaded, pointing to where Jim held Dean motionless while he punched the younger man almost at will. "He'll kill Dean!"

The Forest Service pilot was running over to them before she had finished talking. He was not young, but he was big, with powerful shoulders bulging his jacket. He looked hard and fit.

He grabbed the back of Jim Badger's coat collar and lifted.

"All right! That's enough. Let the kid alone before you kill him."

Badger jerked free. "Keep out of this!" His fist caught the service pilot in the chest.

But this time, Jim had picked the wrong man. The pilot's hard knuckles exploded against Badger's jaw, all the weight of those powerful shoulders in the blow. Jim dropped face down, as Dean struggled to his feet.

Vicki looked at Jim without pity. Dean was shakily wiping his face.

"Thanks! You're the fire warden, aren't you?" Dean panted. "This fire was deliberately set—and Jim Badger set it!"

"How do you know that?" The warden frowned.

"We're sure he did it!" Vicki declared. "We found his hat and tire tracks in the woods just now—we found evidence against him in Charleston—and—and we know his motive!"

"We accuse Jim Badger," Dean added vehemently, "and we want to give our evidence against him!"

"Who are you two?"

"Dean Fletcher, and this is Vicki Barr. Friends of Purnell—this man's unsuspecting partner! We insist you question Jim Badger!"

"All right," said the fire warden, convinced. He pulled his coat back into place. "A man can be arrested on the accusation of a citizen. I have a few questions of my own, too."

Jim groaned and stirred, then pushed himself up on one elbow.

"Get up, Badger," the warden said. "I'm taking you to Slick Pond for informal questioning."

Jim dazedly shook his head. "I can't go to Slick Pond. I've got to stay here. My property's on fire!" As the fire warden dragged Jim into standing position, Jim yelled, "Let me stay here!"

Vicki looked up into the sky and saw other Forest Service planes over the burning tract.

"I've got to stay here! My timber!" Jim shouted. "Go to Slick Pond—because this young snip here—this pup—" He tried to get away from the fire warden.

"Badger, I saw you beating up Fletcher—and that settles it. I'm holding you on charges of assault—and taking you to jail. Get in that red car! You two get in, too. It's all right to leave your Piper Cub right here on the woods road. If the fire spreads any more it will be in the other direction. You can come along and give that testimony of yours to the sheriff."

CHAPTER XV

On Trial

VICKI WAS CONCERNED FOR DEAN. THE BOY'S FACE WAS smeared with blood and dirt, and his hand had a nasty gash on it. But Dean insisted the fight had done him no real harm—"stop fussing over me!"

They drove to Slick Pond in Jim Badger's car, the fire warden at the wheel. Vicki and Dean sat together in the rear seat with the two men's heads unmoving before them. Dean assured Vicki he was all right.

"This breeze is fixing me up. It was a mean fight, though. A dirty fight."

"You've got dirt in that open wound," Vicki worried. "We'll have to get it cleaned and bandaged."

The red car plowed out of the forest and onto dirt road and highway. Vicki pressed her lips tightly together. She could not stop thinking of the cruel and unfair way Jim Badger had fought. To kill.

At the edge of town, a crowd had gathered. They were anxiously watching the reddened sky, up over

Purnell's tract, and the Forest Service planes which flew headlong into the smoke. As the red car drove up, the crowd yelled and milled around, blocking their passage.

"What's up, Warden? Hey! Warden Smith!"

"Jim Badger! Where're yuh goin'?"

"Going to be able to stem that fire, Warden?"

The fire warden angrily blew the horn. "Out of the way! You'll hear about it as soon as we sift out the facts. Let us through!"

The crowd parted and the red car drove slowly down a thronged Main Street. This lumber town, whose livelihood and very existence depended on the forests, had poured out of houses, offices, and mills, even out of school, to watch the red terror up ahead. The roar of flame could be heard faintly even here.

The warden parked the car and ordered them all to enter the jail.

They went into the sheriff's office, a quiet, dusty room. The fire warden drew the sheriff aside and in low tones summarized what had happened, and lodged the complaint. The sheriff's expression did not change as he listened. Like Fire Warden Smith, this police official, MacGregor by name, was powerfully built, a short-spoken, middle-aged man. He closed his office door, motioned them all to take chairs, and said to the fire warden:

"All right, Warden Smith, I have to arrest Badger

on the charge of assault. But you'd better dig up the facts right now on the other charge of fire setting. Get it settled at once. You two, Fletcher and Miss Barr, you're not under arrest, but we'll need your evidence. I understand from Warden Smith that you are lodging the complaints against Badger."

Sheriff MacGregor went to the door, summoned a policeman, and posted him outside their door. Then he said to the fire warden:

"Suppose we do the questioning together."

"Right. I'll start with Badger here."

Jim Badger looked badly frightened. He crossed his legs and tried to resume his usual genial smile. But Dean had done him considerable damage, and the stare of the two officials made him shift in the wooden chair. A strong shaft of daylight from a barred window showed up the fear in Jim's face.

"All right, Badger, we'll come right to the point," the fire warden shot out. "Did you set that fire?"

"Me?" Jim's eyes flew open. "Set a fire on my own property? D'you think I'd deliberately destroy my own timber?"

"Hmm. Who do you think did it, then?"

"Maybe nobody did it. Have you any reason to believe that fire was set?"

The fire warden answered, "Yes, I have reason to think someone started that fire deliberately."

Jim Badger slowly drew himself up in his chair.

"The swine! I'd like to find out who it was! I'd like to get my hands on that vandal who's destroying twenty years of my work!"

"Take it easy, Jim," said Warden Smith. He was unimpressed. "What time were you out in the tract this morning?"

"I wasn't out at the mill until just before you came. I drove out there from Slick Pond at my usual time, I guess around seven-thirty or quarter to eight."

"That's not true," Dean interrupted. "We were flying, and we saw Jim Badger's car parked at the mill at a little after seven."

MacGregor said, "We'll get to you later, Fletcher. Jim, what were you doing at the mill earlier than usual?"

"Going to work for the day! And it wasn't much earlier than usual! For heaven's sakes, you men know me! You've known me for years, know I'm a hard-working, self-respecting lumberman, one of the best in the region."

The two officials' faces softened a little. They exchanged glances, and Sheriff MacGregor said:

"Jim, listen. That fire was set. I agree, it seems unlikely you'd do such a thing. We're not accusing you. We're just asking you."

Jim Badger went on playing the abused innocent. But MacGregor called a break in the questioning. "We want to find a man who saw Badger wearing his hat."

Vicki felt encouraged at that. And in this break she saw an opportunity to have Dean's cuts taken care of.

"Could Dean Fletcher and I go to a doctor, if you don't need us right away for questioning? He needs a little treatment, I think."

"All right. Be back in twenty, thirty minutes."

Once out on the street, Dean scoffed at Vicki's suggestion of a doctor and it was all she could do to get him even to the drugstore. There was too much to see, too much excitement, as word of the fire's progress circulated among the congregated townspeople.

"I don't want to miss anything, either," Vicki said. "But you must get those cuts cleaned. Stop arguing, Dean. It will take only a few minutes."

The druggist washed, medicated and—over Dean's protests—bandaged his hand and jaw. The flier bolted out of the drugstore, Vicki right after him.

They stood at the crowded curb, next to a man who was answering some other people's questions.

"Sure it's a bad fire. Badger could take a loss of thousands on this."

"So could Mr. Purnell," Vicki thought.

"—but the smoke jumpers are doin' their best," the man went on. "I just drove down that road ten minutes ago and it looked to me like the Stony Creek fire, five years back, remember? They got that one under control. So maybe there's hope—"

Vicki had heard enough. She walked with Dean to

the edge of town and the open highway. Traffic was thick there, going to and from the burning tract. News of the fire circulated among the watching townspeople like fire itself.

"Heard they called in extra planes from the National Forest squad."

"Uh-huh. Jed said district rangers too."

"Wal. 'Pears there's a chance."

Vicki and Dean, with the rest, stared at the red-blotted sky. Billowing smoke obscured the treetops and made it impossible to guess which areas were afire and which were still safe. Vicki felt Dean's hand tensely gripping hers. Some men clattered by on horseback, going into Slick Pond. Some of them were forest rangers, soot blackened, and Vicki thought she recognized among them the young man they had met on the lonely hilltop.

"Time to get back to the sheriff's office," Dean said.

They picked their way back through the crowd. Until now Vicki had been too stunned by the fast-moving events of the morning to do anything except react from minute to minute. Now, as she walked, she had a moment for thinking:

Jim Badger must not be allowed to persuade the authorities that he was innocent! Because they knew and trusted him, Jim had an excellent chance of getting off scot free! Something, someone must stop him —or Joan's father would be ruined forever.

A local policeman readmitted them to the sheriff's

office. The office had filled up. The young ranger of the hilltop and two other men were present. Smith and MacGregor were still questioning Jim Badger. He was sweating now, and his ruddy, heavy face in the shaft of light was very red.

"But I'm as innocent as you are, Pop Smith! This is ridiculous!"

The sheriff turned to one of the townsmen in the room.

"Chuck Ferris, Jim comes into your restaurant nearly every morning for breakfast, right?"

"Right. He orders flapjacks, sausages, two cups o' coffee—"

"Never mind that. What time does Jim usually come in?"

"Exackly seven o'clock. Always, wham, right on time!"

"What time did he come in this morning?"

"Say now, I noticed that 'cause I hadn't hardly opened up the place, nor filled up the coffee urn—"

"What time was it, Chuck?"

Chuck Ferris grinned broadly and shuffled his feet. "Jim came in at a quarter to six, and he ate flapjacks, sausages, and two cups—"

"Did he wear his hat?"

"Yes, sir, he did. Always wears his hat."

"Could you identify the hat?"

"Why, it's the one settin' on your desk." The burned hat Vicki and Dean had found in the woods.

And Jim Badger had no other hat to show, now.

"Thanks, Chuck, you can go back to your restaurant." The sheriff turned to the second townsman, but Jim Badger interrupted:

"What are you trying to prove, Mac? Can't a fellow lose his hat or change his habits by a few minutes without being up for trial?"

"Sure, Jim, sure," MacGregor said blandly. "Anyhow, this is no regular trial. It's just that we're going to have to question a lot of people, to find out who set this fire, and it's only logical to question the owner first. If we didn't, the town would be asking *us* questions. Now then, Neelie."

Neelie was an old man, a watchman at one of the mills which was located between Slick Pond and the Badger tract.

"I ain't seed nuthin', suh."

"You saw Jim Badger drive by?"

"Allus sees him drive by. In that red car."

"Was he wearing his hat this morning?"

"Yes, suh. That hat ovah on the desk, suh." Neelie pointed.

The young forest ranger was questioned next. The fire warden addressed him, almost affectionately, as Douglas. He looked, in his forest garments, too big and brown for this musty room.

"Well, Douglas?" the fire warden asked. "Have you a report?"

"Yes, Warden Smith. I was on duty at the lookout station atop Blue Hill since daylight. At a little after six o'clock I noticed Badger's red car go down the highway and turn into his tract. A little while later I thought I saw a sign of smoke in his tract, but couldn't be sure. I sent word to the central station to stand by, just as an off-chance warning."

"Very good, Douglas."

"That isn't quite all, Warden. You see, it was almost windless this morning, and you'll recall we had a good rain just three days ago. So there wasn't much chance that this fire started accidentally."

"Still doesn't prove anything!" Jim Badger shouted cockily. He jumped to his feet. "If that fire was set, who did it? Just let me catch him! How's the fire coming, anyhow? What's happening out there on my tract?"

The fire warden answered. "Our men are bringing the fire under control. Most of your tract will be saved. I'm expecting someone in here any minute with a report."

"A report?" Vicki blurted out hopefully. It was the first thing she had said since her and Dean's return. "Then that will show—"

The sheriff said dryly, "Since you're so eager to talk, miss, you can talk to me. What are you and this young fellow doing around these parts?"

Vicki gave their names and addresses, explained that

she was here on behalf of Mr. Purnell, and she and Dean showed credentials to establish their identity. The sheriff and fire warden frowned over these.

"You say you're here for Jim's partner? You don't look like a businesswoman to me."

Vicki explained further, while Jim Badger's lips curled. She felt that she was being disbelieved, and the more she said the more hollow it sounded.

"All right, miss, that will do. We'll take your word for it, for the time being, until we check up on you." The sheriff turned to Dean. "And what's your business in Slick Pond?"

Dean said, "I live in Charleston, own a private plane, and flew Miss Barr up here. We found Badger's hat and tire tracks in the fire area—"

"Just a minute," MacGregor cut him short. "Let's see if you have a pilot's license." Dean produced his license and MacGregor seemed satisfied. Vicki noticed that Badger's face had changed expression at mention of the plane, as if he was thinking of something. Thinking hard.

"You say you saw Jim Badger at the lumber mill the other day," the sheriff stated, "and he gave you the information you wanted. Then why'd you come back this morning?"

"On a hunch," Vicki said breathlessly before Dean could answer. She did not want any mention of Mr. Cargill back in Charleston, and his warning.

Jim said quickly, "They came back here to beat me up, that's why! MacGregor, I want to put in a charge of assault and battery against this Fletcher!"

Dean suddenly turned pale. "You liar. You started that fight. You tried to grab your hat—"

Jim was on his feet, trying to hit out at the boy, trying—Vicki realized—to stop Dean's words. "How do we know," Jim shouted, "that these two strangers didn't start the fire?"

The warden and sheriff restrained Jim and got him back in his chair. Dean had not moved, taut as an arrow. Only a muscle in his lean cheek clenched and unclenched.

Dean said grimly, "Why won't you let me speak?"

"All in good time," the fire warden spoke up. "Mac, that was some fight. Jim was murdering this lad. I don't kid myself I'm any fighter, but it's a good thing I got there when I did."

Vicki breathed a sigh of relief. The fire warden, at least, was going to listen to their story with some degree of belief. But at the sheriff's next words her hopes dropped again.

"Fletcher, or whatever your name is, we don't like strangers coming into our neighborhood and making trouble. Why'd you hit Jim Badger?"

"Because he hit me," Dean replied steadily.

"That's not so!" Jim sneered. "You grabbed my hat away from me and I wanted it back!"

"I *found* your hat near the fire—"

"I'll ask the questions!" MacGregor cut Dean short again. "You'll each get a chance to tell everything you know. But in due order."

Vicki slid back into her chair, fuming and yet downcast. She did not like the way things were going. There was a local loyalty to Jim Badger, while she and Dean were strangers, to be distrusted. She did not doubt that the case would be handled fairly, but she wondered if these men would recognize in their old friend Jim Badger exactly the kind of treacherous man they were dealing with. Vicki and Dean exchanged despairing glances. Dean's hopes, too, were dwindling.

A knock sounded at the door and, before either MacGregor or Smith could open it, a man rushed in. He was a forest ranger, sooty, covered with mud, out of breath.

"Warden Smith! Warden Smith! We've found—proof! That fire—was deliberately set!"

The man leaned panting against the wall. No one spoke. Jim Badger started a gesture, caught himself.

"That fire—" The ranger gulped in a deep breath, then his words poured out. "We just now fought our way through to the spot where the fire started. It was in a stand of hickory—in a partly logged-out area, mind you! Nothing very much but stumps there." He stopped again to catch his breath.

"In a logged-out area, eh?" the fire warden said ominously. "Go on."

The man nodded and wiped his dirt-streaked face. "Yes, sir. Well, we poked around the charred stumps and we found—Corey's got soil samplings, holding them for evidence—we found traces of kerosene on the ground. And we found car tracks—arrow-shaped tire tracks that match the tires on Jim Badger's car!"

"What of it?" Badger cried. "Someone stole my car, that's all! So as to pin the blame on me!"

No one said anything.

Suddenly Jim Badger sprang out of his chair and made for the closed door. MacGregor ran to block his way but it was Dean who ripped his hands away from the doorknob and hurled Jim Badger against the wall. All the men in the room encircled him. He dropped into his chair and buried his face in his hands.

Out of the silence Vicki said tremblingly, "I'd like to tell my story now." And she told, in full detail now, of how Purnell had been cheated, and what she had learned in Charleston—how Badger had sold ash and hickory without Purnell's knowledge, how he had run Purnell into debt with huge freight bills with the connivance of Ganner, the local freight agent, and how he had stated publicly that he was going to buy out his partner.

"Well, Badger?" the sheriff demanded. Pity lay in

MacGregor's face, but his tone was hard. He whispered to Douglas to bring in the stenographer. "Well, Jim? What have you to say to this girl's final evidence?"

Jim bent his big head. He kept his gaze on his hands. "I guess you've got the goods on me," he mumbled.

A startled intake of breath went around the room. MacGregor's face, and even the faces of Warden Smith and the two forest rangers, plainly said, "It can't be true! Jim setting a forest fire? Good old Jim?"

The sheriff prodded him to talk, but Jim Badger was stubborn. The others were too stunned to say anything. At last Vicki took a long breath and stated:

"From the evidence I've collected, I think I have a pretty good idea of what Jim Badger had planned."

"You have?" MacGregor said with interest. "Well, we want to hear it!"

"Jim Badger must have known," Vicki started hesitantly, "that we were on his trail when Dean and I flew over his tract the other day. That's undoubtedly why he followed us to Charleston, to see if we would learn there about his selling ash and hickory behind Mr. Purnell's back—and about his plot to push his partner out of the business. Then when he found out we had evidence against him, there was just one way out of it, one chance, for Jim Badger." Vicki spoke with slow emphasis.

"He had to gamble. He must have hoped," she said,

"that by setting the tract afire he could persuade Mr. Purnell that the entire tract had burned, make him believe there was little or no lumber business left, and thus trick him into selling out in a rush—without business investigations which would reveal those South American sales.

"And I suspect Jim Badger wasn't going to burn *himself* out—he set the fire only in the ash and hickory where it was partially logged out anyway.

"As to how he thought he could explain away the records the Charleston businessmen have, and the questions that would probably come up in the insurance checkup, well—Jim Badger had told so many convincing lies about owning a hickory and ash tract of his own, and had been believed, I suppose, that he could have used that lie again and been believed again.

"The fire was a trick to put Mr. Purnell on the spot —to make him *want* to sell out in a hurry, without asking any questions. Jim Badger gambled on that."

Vicki sank back in her chair. All eyes turned on Jim Badger.

Badger drew himself up. "It was a slick idea, and came darn near succeeding, too." He smiled at his own wiliness. "But there's one part you didn't figure out, Miss Barr. I was going to telephone Purnell this morning, tell him the tract was on fire, and pull the rush act on him to get out of the business in a hurry. I was going to say 'Another man will buy the tract anyway, fire or not, this is without precedent, you can get out and save yourself'—try to stampede Purnell, see? 'Course that other man was me. It would've worked, too, except for this girl." Jim sighed.

Jim Badger was formally charged with setting the forest fire and locked up pending trial.

Vicki went to telephone the whole story long-distance to Mr. Purnell. His voice at the other end of the wire was pathetically bewildered. Vicki reassured him that Jim Badger was caught now, the fire checked, and his business troubles over. Then she remembered that the debt of twenty-five thousand dollars still hung over Mr. Purnell's head.

CHAPTER XVI

Reward

THE ATLANTIC WAS POUNDING ALONG VIRGINIA BEACH, that December afternoon as Vicki and Dean drove along the beach road. Dean had not wanted to accompany Vicki on this, possibly her last visit for a time, to the Purnells.

"I ought to be back in the hangar tuning up Marietta," he fretted, as their taxi bucked the ocean wind. "Besides, I'll be in your way."

"You contributed to solving the Purnells' troubles," Vicki said warmly. "I want them to see that beautiful bandage on your hand—my hero!"

Dean grunted but he looked pleased. The Purnells' brown house hove into view, backed by the tall pines.

"Remember the first time we saw this house, and we saw a young girl come out and run down the beach?" Vicki asked dreamily. "What a lot has happened since then!"

The white door with its brass eagle stood ajar, the

Purnells waited in the doorway. Joan came flying through the dooryard.

"Vicki, Vicki! What a help you've been to us!"

Vicki hugged her in return. The wind blew Joan's gold-brown hair across Vicki's cheek. "Joanie, you'll freeze! Get in the house—I brought Dean!"

"Victoria!" Mr. Purnell limped forward happily, as the three young people trooped in. He shut out the wind and cold behind them. "Vicki, I'm so grateful, I haven't adequate words— And this is your flying friend who has done so much for us!" His gentle eyes glowed at her and Dean.

Mrs. Purnell cried, "I'm so rattlebrained, I don't quite understand it all—but I do know you did something wonderful!" and kissed Vicki with feeling.

Dean grinned and muttered, "Vicki is an old, reliable firm," while the Purnells crowded around her. Vicki drew Dean forward, saying he had helped immensely, and it was Dean's turn to flush at the Purnells' attentions.

In their gratitude was pathos. It showed in Mr. Purnell's moist eyes, in Joan's look of intense relief. Mrs. Purnell's irritability had vanished and she smiled like a beautiful child.

They came into the pine-paneled living room with its bird prints. Mrs. Purnell blurted out:

"We have the loan. Vicki—Dean—we have the loan!"

Vicki let out a cry of joy. "When—how— Then everything's all right?"

Mr. Purnell beamed. "Mr. Roland, the banker, finally returned and he's granted me the full twenty-five-thousand-dollar loan. Yes, everything is all right—here, and especially at Slick Pond. Thanks to you, Victoria!"

Joan's eyes turned very dark and soft. "Thank you, Vicki. Thank you."

Vicki spoke her happiness and good wishes for the Purnell family from the bottom of her full heart. She caught Dean looking at her thoughtfully, with a foolish expression on his face. That must be Dean's romantic expression, Vicki guessed. But all her own feelings were focused on Joan and her parents. It was wonderful that they were safe and secure once more.

Mr. Purnell was insisting that she and Dean sit down and give them a blow-by-blow account of how she had fathomed Jim Badger's plottings.

They all listened eagerly. In the lovely room the facts sounded violent and incongruous—as out of place as if Jim Badger himself had been standing here, grinning all over his ruddy face. Mr. Purnell could hardly believe what Vicki told. He shook his scholarly head and by the time Vicki finished he was very sober.

"What a terrible ruin you saved us from, Victoria."

"What a terrible situation, and what a terrible man,"

Mrs. Purnell exclaimed, "for a gentle, helpless little girl like Vicki to get mixed up with!"

Joan giggled. "I'd say Vicki isn't so helpless."

"I had Dean to help me," Vicki reminded them.

Dean grinned at her. "Any time."

They smiled at each other warmly.

Mr. Purnell asked Vicki a few more questions about business details. Vicki assured him that his tract had suffered no serious loss, that thanks to the Forest Service only the partly logged-out areas had burned. She produced the map of the Purnell tract and showed him the exact extent of the damage, and exactly what grew on his land.

"Better than I had hoped for," Joan's father said. "From now on, Joan is going to help me. And—this is really good news!—our Miss Spry is coming back to us! Her doctor has given her his permission to return. A rest did wonders for her. As soon as Miss Spry arrives, I am going down to Charleston and ask your Mr. Cargill, Vicki, to recommend an honest foreman to run my lumber mill. And while I'm there I'll spend some time with the new freight agent who will be in charge in Ganner's place. Incidentally, I shall take steps to see that Ganner is punished for what he's done. I've already talked to the railroad people about it. And after this, now that Miss Spry is coming back to take over the Norfolk work, I shall make frequent trips to Slick Pond and keep an eye on things!"

Joan said gently, "Why, Dad, if you don't watch out, you'll turn into a businessman."

Carter Purnell smiled. "I shall never be much of a businessman, I'm afraid. But it's thanks to Vicki that I still have a business at all."

"It's thanks to Vicki," Mrs. Purnell said joyously, "that we're all together and happy once more."

Vicki squirmed. Dean said, teasing, "You make her sound like a heroine."

"She is," said Mr. Purnell, smiling.

CHAPTER XVII

Home Base

VICKI AND DEAN FLEW BACK FROM NORFOLK TO NEW York, leaving Monday morning on the commercial airliner, after being guests of the Purnells overnight. They arrived at the New York airport around noon, none too soon. The air promised snow, ceiling and visibility were dropping, and from the activity on the field, Vicki realized that scheduled flights were being canceled.

"Too bad," Dean said as they walked across the windy airfield, dodging trucks dragging planes back to the hangars. "Maybe my flight tonight will be canceled, too. I wouldn't mind, I'm kind of tired. How about you, Vic?"

"I'm pretty tired, too," she confessed. "And while I'm sorry to see flights canceled, still, it means the girls will be grounded and at the apartment. I'd enjoy a good visit with them."

Vicki was secretly relieved at the flight cancellations for another reason. This was the day when her

204

week of suspension was up. Today she had to report to Ruth Benson and learn whether she was still in disgrace with the superintendent, even though her week of suspension was over. He might forever think her incompetent because of that one slip. The dirty weather might put off that dreaded interview a few hours longer.

At the hangar, Dean stopped. "I'd like to stop in and see Captain Jordan and have a look at the ships."

"Thought you were tired!" Vicki smiled. She knew Dean was never too tired for the love of his life: planes.

"Uh—want to come in with me for a few minutes? Then I'll take you home, Vic."

"I'd better not, Dean. I have to see Miss Benson," Vicki said rather unhappily. She held out her hand, and looked at the tall young flier with affection in her blue eyes. "Thank you for everything," she said simply.

Dean got fussed, pumped her hand, patted her on the shoulder, said, "Not at all, not at all," and strode into the hangar before Vicki could embarrass him any further. Grinning, she turned away, and started off determinedly for the office of the assistant superintendent of flight stewardesses.

That handsome young woman studied Vicki across her desk. "I won't keep you on tenterhooks, Vicki. Your suspension is not going to be held against you."

"Oh!" Vicki blew out a big sigh of relief. "That's a load off my mind!"

Miss Benson, still regarding Vicki with her level glance, continued: "Vicki, why didn't you explain to the superintendent why you missed the plane from Chicago that evening? Saving a young sister from possible drowning is an extenuating circumstance which even an airline would accept. Heavens, child! Why didn't you tell us you were a heroine? I found out too late to do anything about it, even if I'd been here. You should have told him. I don't know whether he could have overlooked your failure to wire that you had missed the plane—that's a breach of the regulations every stewardess knows about. But it would have helped. You are too proud, Vicki, for your own good sometimes.

"However," Miss Benson said consolingly, "that nice letter to the airline from Mr. Purnell, and your taking good care of his daughter, have gone into your record. I put them in." She grinned at Vicki. "I understand the superintendent practically ate you alive. I don't think he will again. I've talked to him about you."

Vicki looked into Ruth Benson's brilliant gray eyes, and sat speechless with gratitude.

"In fact, Vicki," Miss Benson went on, "aside from that one slip, you do very nice work. You're one of my best girls. I'd like to see you take a Spanish test—right now—with an eye to that Mexican assignment."

"A Spanish test? Now—when I'm unprepared and rusty?" Vicki gasped. "Oh, Miss Benson, would I really have a chance to get to Mexico?"

Ruth Benson simply handed her a questionnaire to fill out, and then sent her next door to the office of Federal's Pan-American supervisor. Vicki's head was already in a whirl, and when Mr. Robles smilingly greeted her with, "*¿Cómo está? Siéntese y hable conmigo.*"—"How do you do? Sit down and talk to me"— Vicki's mind went absolutely blank.

But Mr. Robles was kind and encouraging—in Spanish. Gradually Vicki found herself chatting away in Spanish with him, eagerly asking whether Mexico City really was New York, Paris, and Madrid all rolled into one gay and enchanting city. Mr. Robles said—in Spanish—yes, it was, and told Vicki her Spanish was quite good.

"You haven't even an accent," he said in surprise.

Vicki was pleased, but Mexico seemed a remote hope. Just now she was more anxious to know when she could resume her Norfolk run. She popped into Miss Benson's office again.

"But I'm not putting you back on the Norfolk run," Ruth Benson said. "I haven't decided yet where to place you."

"Then I'm to have a new assignment? Oh, fun!"

The handsome young woman twinkled at Vicki across her desk.

"I never saw such a glutton for change as you are, Vicki Barr!"

"Please tell me where I'm going next. Please!"

"We haven't made up the new flight schedules for

the first of the year yet. You go home to Fairview and rest until I send for you."

Vicki wailed, "I won't be able to rest for wondering!"

"You wouldn't be able to rest if I were able to tell you. Scat, now, and let me work!"

Vicki did a great deal of excited speculating all the way back to the apartment.

For once, everyone was at home. There were shrieks and a scramble as Vicki unlocked the front door, and cries of "Don't let her in!"

"Why not, for goodness' sake?" Vicki demanded. "I live here!"

Mrs. Duff put her plump finger to her lips. "Christmas presents, dearie. And don't trip on the tissue paper."

A regular snowstorm of tissue paper covered the apartment. Vicki had nearly forgotten, in her concern over the Purnells, that Christmas was only two weeks off. From under the biggest heap of tissue paper and bright wrappings, Jean Cox poked her cropped head.

"Vicki, my love!" Jean got up off her hands and knees. "Are you what Santa brought me? It's about time you came back to roost! Did you have fun? How was Slick Pond?"

Little Celia Trimble ran in. "Do I hear Vicki? We've missed you! What about your trip? Was it exciting?"

"I'll tell you all about it later, Celia. How are the babies?"

"Wonderful! They're assigning me to the Baby Plane —with hammocks and toys and everything!"

"Celia's the only one of us," Jean exclaimed, "who isn't studying Spanish—or taking Spanish exams. Everyone's hoping to get one of those two Mexico jobs!"

Redheaded Dot, striding in, ordered, "Don't even mention babies! That's all we hear around here—that, Spanish verbs, and Mexican idioms. We take our Spanish tests this afternoon. How are you, Vicki?"

Charmion and Tessa came in then. Seeing Vicki, Tessa cried, "Let's give a party! We're hardly ever all home at the same time! Doesn't that call for a celebration?"

Charmion smiled gently at Vicki, and kissed her on the very tip of her nose. "Had to hide your Christmas presents before I could come out and say hello. Yes, let's do have a little party. Just among ourselves."

"Don't forget to ask Pete Carmody!" Jean blurted out. She flushed. "Girls, I have a secret to confess. I— I like him."

They howled with laughter. Jean's secret had been obvious for weeks.

They called up Dean and Pete, The Three Bears, and a few other friends. Enlisting Mrs. Duff's willing aid, they set up a buffet table, turned on the radio, and danced and talked until very late that night.

Vicki flew home to Fairview the following day. As always, it thrilled her to travel by air, and to travel as a passenger (with Federal's compliments) was pure luxury. The flight to Chicago was all too brief to suit her. At Chicago, her father was unable to meet her with the car, because some of the roads were snowbound. She took the rattle-bang local train down to Fairview, chatting with old Mr. Stark, the conductor, who had been her friend since she was six.

The Castle stood like a storybook house in its garden of snow. Vicki, coming up the curving driveway in a cab, raised her eyes to the tower and to the blue-curtained windows which were hers. At the oaken door, among the frost and evergreen, bloomed one splendid Christmas rose.

Her family was waiting at The Castle's door. Vicki had forgotten a little how handsome, what darlings, they were. Why, of all the people she had been seeing, her own family was the very nicest!

Her father bent to kiss her and said with a mock-professorial air, "Freckles has lodged a complaint about your absence. The rest of us don't care, of course."

Vicki fell into her mother's arms. Betty Barr looked her over, and with a lively toss of her curls declared that "flying agrees with our Vicki! No wonder you seldom come home. I wouldn't either!"

"You're just in the nickel of time," Ginny squealed. "We're going to—"

"That's nick, sweetie, not nickel, and how's my pet sister?"

"Fine, and we're going to Tootsie Miller's party, and you're invited, and Dickie Brown wants to call for you!"

Freckles, bounding around her feet, seemed to think all this homecoming and festivity a very fine idea.

Vicki was still standing there in the foyer, chattering away delightedly with her family, when the doorbell rang. It was a messenger, bringing a telegram for her. The telegram came from Ruth Benson, and it read: "A LITTLE EARLY BUT HERE'S YOUR CHRISTMAS PRESENT, VICKI. YOU'RE GOING TO MEXICO. CONGRATULATIONS!"

VICKI BARR continues her exciting adventures in the next volume, THE HIDDEN VALLEY MYSTERY. Don't miss this thrilling, colorful story of Mexico and how Vicki unravels the mystery of the stolen historic antiques.